SNAKES' NEST

Lêdo Ivo is one of Brazil's most prolific and controversial authors. As a poet, Ivo has published fifteen volumes of poetic monographs and collections, spanning the years from 1944–1976. Interested readers may find his collected poems, *Central Poética* (Rio: Aguilar, 1976), in specialized libraries in the United States. *La imaginaria ventana abierta,* an anthology of Ivo's poems translated by Carlos Montemayor, was published by Premiá of Mexico in 1980. The author has two new volumes of poetry (written between 1970 and 1979) awaiting publication in Brazil: *O Soldado Raso (The Common Soldier)* and *A Noite Misteriosa (The Mysterious Night).*

In prose, Ivo has published three novels (two of which have won prizes), two collections of short stories, a satirical novelette, and ten volumes of literary and polemical essays, the most recent of which (1979) is entitled *Confessions of a Poet. Snakes' Nest* won the coveted Walmap prize in 1973. (The Walmap is a prestigious novel competition in which entries are submitted anonymously and judged by a distinguished panel of authors and critics.) Ivo's long fascination with American and European literature has resulted in several distinguished translations, among which may be found those of Jane Austen, Guy de Maupassant, Rimbaud (a passion since adolescence) and Dostoevski. Ivo is also beguiled by Melville and Hawthorne, interests he shares with another South American author, Jorge Luis Borges. His devotion to Dashiell Hammett and Raymond Chandler may in part be responsible for the "mystery novel" approach used in *Snakes' Nest.*

J. M. T.

SNAKES' NEST

or

A Tale Badly Told

A Novel by Lêdo Ivo

TRANSLATED BY KERN KRAPOHL,
WITH AN INTRODUCTION
BY JON M. TOLMAN

A NEW DIRECTIONS BOOK

TRANSLATOR'S ACKNOWLEDGMENTS

I sincerely thank Jane Cooper and Prof. Jon Tolman, who mixed critical judgment and kind suggestions in just the right proportion to keep the translator from embarrassing himself on numerous occasions. Special mention must be made of Kerry Shawn Keys, good friend and poet. Without his unflagging support and tireless efforts this translation would never have seen the light of day.

K. K.

Copyright © 1973, 1980 by Lêdo Ivo
Copyright © 1981 by Lêdo Ivo and Kern Krapohl
Copyright © 1981 by Jon M. Tolman

Ninho de Cobras (Snakes' Nest) originally appeared in Brazil in 1973; this English language edition is published by arrangement with the author.

Manufactured in the United States of America
First published clothbound and as New Directions Paperbook 521 in 1981

Published simultaneously in Canada by George J. McLeod, Ltd., Toronto

Library of Congress Cataloging in Publication Data

Ivo, Lêdo.
    Snakes' nest, or, A tale badly told.
    (A New Directions Book)
    Translation of: Ninho de cobras.
    I. Title.
PO9697.I9N513   1981   869.3   81–3956
ISBN 0–8112–0806–0   AACR2
ISBN 0–8112–0807–9 (pbk.)

New Directions Books are published for James Laughlin
by New Directions Publishing Corporation,
80 Eighth Avenue, New York 10011

êdo Ivo gained national attention with his first collection of poems, *As Imaginações* (*Imaginations*, 1944), and has since gone on to publish more than sixteen volumes of poetic monographs and collections. He rapidly became an articulate and outspoken defender of a revisionist aesthetics, collectively known in Brazil as the "Generation of 1945," which rejected the prevailing modernist notions of poetry. In spite of his identification with the aforementioned generation, Ivo's poetry may perhaps be characterized by the term "transgression:" a highly idiosyncratic vision of the world, expressed by a unique style that toys with the limits of poetic diction, infringing upon and violating the norms. It is a poetry of extremes and extremely varied moods and attitudes. At one end of Ivo's poetic spectrum are long, sprawling odes expressed in a grandiloquent style that represents a conscious importation of tropical regionalism into Brazil's temperate southern zone. At the other end are short, pithy poems (often sonnets) that are concerned with commonplace things and places, with specificity of smell, feel and appearance.

So much attention to poetry may seem a digression in an introduction to a novel, but it seems to me that *Snakes' Nest* is in many ways similar to Ivo's poetic works: there is the intensely poetic, rambling, apparently inept narration that masks a heterodoxical attitude toward established forms. There is the love of place, in all its ugliness. There is the love of language and rhetoric, and finally, a mystery novel format that masks a rather straightforward preoccupation with human destiny and the meaning of life. The author himself has refused to call *Snakes' Nest* a novel: "One day that fox I saw killed as a child, the symbol of the night, of dreams and liberty, would emerge, transfigured, from the depths of my unconsciousness to become a character, perhaps the major character, of a story, *Snakes' Nest*, that I did not dare to call a novel. In this I was sensitive to the evidence that we live in an aesthetic epoch marked by the emergence of hybrid genres or nameless texts." Thus, we have *Snakes' Nest*, ambiguous in both form and content: a transgressional novel.

Certain features of *Snakes' Nest* would seem to demand a short explanation. The novel is set in the early 40s, during what in Brazil was known as the "New State," a semi-fascist experiment in *caudillismo* that lasted from 1930 to 1945. Getúlio Vargas, the caudillo, was a charismatic leader from southern Brazil with definite similarities to his better-known Argentine neighbor, Juan Perón. Although responsible for modernizing Brazil's society and institutions (the so-called First Republic was run by a landed oligarchy), Vargas presided over a regime that flirted with the Axis, countenanced a pervasive censorship, and imprisoned numerous writers and intellectuals. There was also a cult of personality, and the pictures on the walls of Maceió in the novel are those of the dictator.

The Maceió portrayed in the novel is that of the author's childhood, and he has used its seedy opulence (although a state capital and seaport, Maceió has been by-passed by the forces of modernization located in Recife to the north and Salvador to the south) as the setting for his examination of good and evil. The reader should keep in mind that the novel was written and published during another period of dictatorship in Brazil, one even more repressive than that which frames the events narrated. Certain inevitable but implicit parallels are thereby established for Brazilian readers of this allegorical tale. The American reader can perhaps imagine such a tale emerging from Vichy, France, or some other marginal dictatorship. In this case, the national corruption has a backwater counterpart, a decadent city in which all the ills of society are manifest. As a microcosm of violence and corruption, the Maceió of the novel perhaps has its parallels in certain redneck villages of the Faulknerian south.

If I have emphasized the universal aspects of this novel, I should also mention its Brazilian qualities. The setting is quite specifically Brazilian provincial, although the Maceió of *Snakes' Nest* has resemblances to such Latin American ports as Tampico or Callao. The exotic appeal of such a place to the American reader is in many ways the same as that for a reader from Rio or São Paulo for whom Maceió is as remote and foreign as Bangkok.

Before closing this introduction to an artfully achieved "poorly told tale," I should like to propose that *Snakes' Nest* makes an intriguing contribution to the literature of the unreliable narrator. Is the pompous, bumbling narrator, so full of local history and colorful details, really the snitch? Does the novel end with a murder? Because of the narrator's ineptness the reader is left confused. Although he has learned a great deal about the characters and events of the novel, he ultimately must resign himself to the same kind of moral uncertainty that marks all our human endeavors. We know in part, we speak in part, we conceal in part, ultimately possessing no better knowledge of ourselves than we do of our fellow man.

I think it is appropriate, in this preface to a translation, to give the last word to the author himself. In a reaction to the preceding paragraph in a draft version, Ivo pointed out that in a dictatorship, all narration becomes unreliable:

Regarding the figure of the unreliable narrator, I think it is true that during a dictatorship, all narrations are poorly told, since a dictatorship is the Kingdom of Lies and cannot tolerate the truth. How can one tell the truth or tell a truthful story in a regime of terror, persecution, and the destruction of the individual? On the other hand, the narrative technique employed in this novel is that of horsethieves and gypsies, liars *par excellence*. You know that we are all mythographers, creators of fictions, which, of course, leaves those writers who are so dedicated to documenting reality in a real fix. In such conditions I feel myself absolved from the sin of considering fiction a universe parallel to the real world.

> Jon M. Tolman
> The University of New Mexico

> . . . destiny generally signifies an inevitable process which goes forward regardless of the will of God or man.
>
> SAINT AUGUSTINE

That night a fox had come down to the center of the city. She'd come from the woods, where even at night the trees held the summer heat in their dry branches. After passing through an area of deformed shrubs she left behind the brush and twigs which sometimes snapped dully in the darkness.

She halted near the tableland where the Americans had constructed the airport at the beginning of the war, and her eyes, immune to dreams and desolation, fixed for an instant on the red lights of the landing strip. After a moment's vigilance, she chose the wider road and descended toward the city. She crouched tightly against a farm fence when the lights of an old truck, straining and dripping oil, lit the dusty road of compacted earth, then continued on her way, crossing deserted streets and avenues lined by bungalows engulfed in somber gardens. Only the street lights shone. The dropping of a pottery tree fruit momentarily filled the night's silence, as if a star fragment had fallen to earth. A centipede took refuge in a pile of rotten timbers, dissolving in the darkness of the rubble.

The fox reached the first cobblestone street, angled across some streetcar tracks, descended Martyrs' Lane, and began to wander the narrow streets of the city's center. In the darkness she seemed a stray dog, but from the moment she had appeared on a shortcut through the thick brush until she had reached Main Street, not a single human eye had spied her or had paused to consider her, not even to confuse her with a flea-ridden, ownerless cur. Nor did she evidence fright, astuteness, or curiosity.

The houses slept, and seemed greatly diminished, even those of more than one story. The men and women slept. Smelling of sweat, of sperm, of the sugar which for centuries had flowed from the countryside, of any secretion whatsoever, they slept in the glassy night, dreaming and tossing about while bats swung like lamps from the rafters, mosquitoes buzzed, and rats and cockroaches moved uninhibitedly about in the darkness.

And there outside in the street, still and oppressive though not far from the waves, the fox stalked. As if the sea's spongy odor had drawn her, she continued descending streets until reaching the water's edge. For the first time her feet felt the sweetness of sand on the beach.

She drew near the ocean, letting a wave's thin edge wet her feet, not seeing the blue tinged whiteness of the clouds. She felt the stunning coolness of the living water on her dry nails. Curving her muzzle, she stretched her quivering, thirsty tongue toward it, but quickly jerked back in a movement of nausea and vertigo. The breaking of the waves seemed to disturb her.

She moved away from the ocean and continued along the beach toward the dark bulk of warehouses which, smelling of sugar even at night—when all the depots were closed and there was no loading or unloading to be done—advanced toward the sea, supported by green-black pilings which presumably would never rot, but would enter eternity with all their immemorial solidity. (Nearby, beneath one of the houses, the English seamen were buried. Many years before, a ship had anchored in the port of Jaraguá with plague on board. The cadavers of the mariners, dead of yellow fever, had been taken ashore and interred on the beach, which with the passage of time became an avenue, leveling their tombs. And on certain nights, when there are English ships anchored in the harbor, the souls of these sailors wander through Jaraguá's deserted streets, looking for ferrymen to carry them on board and leave them to rest beneath the same flag which sheltered them in the days when, shipping out on the doomed craft, they'd dreamed of the green tropics, of coconut palms, parrots, canaries, and dusky women.) The fox paused next to an upturned barge. Perhaps she sniffed at its hull, which days before had been repainted and smelled of tar. A crab brushed her with its left front claw.

Moments later she stopped in front of the steps of the Chamber of Commerce and contemplated the white columns of the building which projected itself against the blackness of the night like a milky and virginal shadow. She went so far as to climb two or three steps. Some yards away in the Western office, a telegraph operator was awake, and he lightly kept his vigil, sweet like sleep itself, in the yellowed air of the room. His gaze fixed on a pamphlet's illustrations, he awaited the chance signals which, through submarine cables, were crossing the grainy night of the depths where no star sparkled.

With a rapid movement, the fox changed direction and went down a street smelling of sugar and onions. (Behind the closed doors of the leprous storefronts, ulcerated by the seawind, lay sacks of sugar, Indian hemp and onions, bales of cotton, cheap sugarcane rum, corn, coconuts, and textile fibers.)

Despite the nearness of the tumescent sea, which sent forth into the nearby streets the odor of departure and decay—the

disconcerting mixture of voyage and corruption which, lo-
cating itself on an indecisive and fluctuating line, could as
easily be accumulated garbage as the stench of slimy ocean
wastes—despite this nearness of salt and ship, of seaweed and
shellfish, the streets possessed a terrestrial quality, heavy and
lifeless. It was as if there, in those buildings with their rusty
iron gratings and in the twisted and sloping sidewalks, man
had set himself to erect his first and most resistant bulwark
against the sea and departure, raising a monument that even
at night smelled of merchandise and profit. And the closed
windows hid love and hate, atonement and terror, adultery
and sodomy. Day and night, clocks measured the flow of
tedium and senseless waiting.

The fox paused once more, recognizing in the air a vague
and vaporous smell of leather, which then changed to that of
molasses. Perhaps she was remembering, at that moment, a
certain time in her life when her nostrils had discovered the
odor of the perennial rivers which fertilized the marshy
banks of the place where she had been born. But she would
have been unable to say if the instant when she had inherited
the perception of her native environment had occurred
during the day, beneath the sun which makes the wax palms
tremble, or if at night, when the earth drinks the clarity of
the stars. Also, it would have been impossible for her to
discern whether in that remote moment she had lived in the
Forest Zone, where the canefields had grown up in place of
the immemorial woods, swept clean by fire, and where the
Indians, persecuted by the colonists, had disappeared; or if
that moment already dead had dissolved into itself in another
landscape, among saguaro cactus and ground lilies. Now she
felt the sea wind caressing her back, and all her past moments
melted together and slid away.

Alternating between astuteness and confusion, the fox returned to the center of the city, going down other narrow
streets. Certainly, this zigzag roaming of a half dark horizon

gave her a general view of Maceió, although she had not gone as far as the shore of the lagoon or even approached the two cemeteries. While coming down the hillside, after passing the farms, the houses surrounded by gardens, and the bungalows, she had seen the Government Palace from the other side of the church. The lacerated signboard of the Rex Movie Theater (it was the old Floriano where many years past, businessmen, lawyers, doctors, government employees consumed by debts, ranchers, and assassins had laughed after dinner, watching Chaplin comedies and seeing the Mack Sennett bathing beauties sink evanescently behind the dunes of an almost sepia sea, when they weren't being captivated by the spectacle of a dimly projected snowfield), a notary public's sign, the Great Western Company's train already resting in the station, waiting for the passengers who at dawn would depart for Recife, the police barracks, a blind alley called the Sheep's Armpit, the jail, Saint Vincent's Hospital, the Deodoro Theater, the statues of Marshals Deodoro da Fonseca and Floriano Peixoto—who inspired in the Alagoans the glorious feeling that the country owed them not only the proclamation, but the consolidation of the Republic as well—Sin Street (where the whores finally slept in rooms smelling of lotion), all this went filing by the fox's eyes, and it was allowable that she felt, in the most intellectual and illuminated part of her instinct, that she was exploring a city, the first and only city she was to know in all her life.

In the police barracks, a sentry, yawning from drowsiness, saw the fox moving at a distance, but it never crossed his mind that he might be dealing with any creature other than a stray dog. A few windows were lit up in Saint Vincent's Hospital. One had swung open at the exact instant the fox reached the opposite sidewalk, but the sister who had unlatched it in order to spy for a moment on the motionless desolation of the night, so like her vigil, hadn't seen the animal skulking toward the corner. The sister suffered from insomnia. She'd opened *her* window (as she often said to herself) for an early morning instant, and had stayed to contemplate the darkness, limpid yet oppressive, which comes before the dawn. The breeze coming from the nearby ocean, cooling her face, seemed to liberate her of everything within, of acceptance and waiting, renunciation and perplexity—a personal emptiness filled everyday by livid faces mortified by illness.

Minutes later the fox felt in her nostrils the scent of blood and raw meat. She was crossing the square directly in front of the Municipal Market, which smelled of fruits and the slaughterhouse. But suddenly this nauseating stench was replaced by a distant yet noticeable ocean smell. And from very far away, from reefs of sand and coral, from mangroves and coastal pools where crabs were sleeping, from coconut groves lashed constantly by the wind, from canefields advancing to the edge of the sea, from riverbanks overgrown by sedge, there came an odor which, through the cracks of the roofs, penetrated the houses and permeated the people's dreams. To the sleep of each one, to the inadmissible fraction of dream, there was added this aroma of the dying night. It was perhaps a perfume of flowering cashew, or the leaf of an auricuri palm rhythmically struck by the breeze. And this smell coming from everywhere, from the bottom of caves, from dunes and creeks, from naked beaches, from inundated fields, from valleys and lagoons, mixed with the sleep of the people, with what within them was most human, earthy and vital—ambition, mendacity, adultery, or a certain cruelty most conspicuous in sultry weather, as if it were fed by the blind luminosity of the soft full day.

The fox, confusedly remembering a river which never ran dry, observed that the darkness was diminishing. A jasmine shrub trembled, hidden by a wall. Banana trees rustled. Chickens stirred in backyards. Roosters crowed. Dirty house fronts, washed in vain by rain squalls, were becoming clearer.

Even the wall of the mortuary, where there was only one corpse—a drowned teamster whom the sea had thrown up, monstrously round and swollen with a whirling life of water —promised a radiant clarity as soon as daybreak came. Dogs barked. She stalked, and it was as if she explored less the perspective unfolding translucently before her eyes than the thick substance of the very moment. Her ash colored eyes, intensely animal-like, without the gift of remembering but only of recognition, didn't recall the oven for the making of lime which she'd seen one morning near a plantation manor, nor the manioc root encountered occasionally in chalky soil and sniffed with indifference. She remembered nothing—and in front of her was the moment, glassy like quartz, a material perhaps capable of injuring feet and tail. Like a dog, she crouched to urinate by a wall where a protest had been scrawled the night before: *Down with the New State!* Down with the dictatorship!*

In that second of time in which the fox's piss formed a small triangle on the house wall and ran down the sidewalk, Professor Serafim Gonçalves was not dreaming in the extremely wide bed which sheltered his body, turned even fatter by sleep. He was only sleeping, a deep sleep, snoring; and it was as if there existed neither his fatness nor the special appeals which had been before the Supreme Court for years, neither the faces of his clients nor his pupils. At his side, thin, fine, her body defined by muscle and bone, his wife shivered, hugging the chamomile pillow. She was dreaming, but it was an unformed scribble of a dream which could never raise itself to the category of a narrative.

With her bladder relieved, the fox continued roaming about the dark and deserted city. The sky was reddening,

* The Vargas dictatorship (1937–1945). Vargas centralized power in the executive, closed the congress, and replaced the state governors with appointed interventors.

the outlines of windows and doors and soot-covered porches were becoming clearer on the house fronts worn by the tropical rains.

Rude calendars of time in the gloom, things proclaimed the century, the year, the day. In the closed registries lay the paper histories of the city: births, inventories, marriages, all the dusty and unending chronicle of thousands of sedentary destinies which time was bleeding away, files of names without importance or meaning, without faces and without voices, like the street stones and the tiles torn loose from terrace walls which the inclement weather was slowly wearing away. And from the pulp of a pottery tree fruit, crushed falling in a schoolyard, there emanated a penetrating perfume, rival of childhood.

The fox, barely aware of the hour's passing despite her measuring of life by the cadenced, uninterrupted succession of days and nights, knew that dawn was breaking. The renewed strength of the roosters' crowing and the flame-colored blotches which striped the horizon and advanced along the decrepit walls announced the sunrise. Feeling thirsty, she stopped and drank from a puddle which reflected the pallor of a glassy sky. Having gone round the wall of a school, she went up the street on the left-hand side, across from the wall guarding the Government Palace gardens.

In the silence, the cock crowed. It was a cock of golden plumage, resplendent, and his blood red comb rivaled the flaming glory of the dawn. Magnificent, exultant, he sang joyously in the splendor of the awakening day, rousing the Federal Interventor and the magistrates, the whores and the saints, proclaiming the wonder of the morning while his spurs raked the entire earth.

It was then, at the police station, that a guard discovered the fox with his goggling eyes and recognized her as if she were the prized and never obtained relic of his childhood. He called to a companion and pointed her out. The other, cleaning the sleep from his eyes with his fingers, was still doubtful. But it was a fox! Suddenly the animal felt itself menaced and pursued. She had fallen into a trap, and both in front and behind, palisades were being raised. Like all animals, she didn't believe in her own death; she judged herself immortal, even though she accepted her immortality with the bland indifference of a being without metaphysics.

The certainty, though, was that she was being chased, in the city which was awakening little by little, and in whose native silence the widest variety of sounds was stirring (and water boiled in teapots, or ran from recently opened faucets, and bread came forth from crackling ovens, and the nun who suffered with insomnia approached the bed where an old woman with swollen eyes was dying, and a butcher's bloody knife tore at what had formerly been the chest of a steer, and a priest, sitting on the edge of a bed, was tying his shoelaces, and a green-eyed mulatto, at Dina's, had her sleep disturbed by the whistling of a ship). It was the morning breaking, and the sky, turning momentarily lilac, was entirely too high to hear the cries of a few men pursuing a fox. And she, with her ash-colored eyes and a suppleness inherited from her ancestors, accustomed to persecutions much more tenacious and cruel, was confusedly possessed by the notion that she found herself between existence and nothing, as some minutes before she had felt herself between thirst and water. Shortly, her conviction of danger became more urgent. Men were approaching her, grotesque as scarecrows, their animal snouts open in expressions of impious happiness, carrying lethal instruments which were bound to strike her.

And in a wisp of time, much less than that in which a sliver of star slides in the blind dark sky, the fox knew death, something stunning and brilliant which could only be death, if it exists at all in its absurd fullness and harsh magnificence, and isn't solely a fiction or point of reference for those living, who suddenly stop hating and loving, dismissed so quickly from all their greatness and misery. It was death which, incandescent and perverse, reached her, changing her undeniable animal beauty, agitating her blood, turning glassy her vision of the crystalline and wraithlike morning.

Disfigured by the blows the men had rained down upon her, she lay for more than an hour on the cobblestones, a formless lump of meat and bloodsoaked hair, and the curious took their turns in a circle around her, exchanging the most varied comments. When the day was finally clearing for good, a garbage wagon stopped near the throng, and the fox's body was thrown onto the pile of rubbish.

THE PROFESSOR

"**A** fox, right in the heart of the city! And they still say that Maceió is a civilized place," remarked Professor Serafim Gonçalves at the door of the Colombo Bar, after motioning away a beggar wearing an auricuri palm leaf hat.

Though it was habitually said that Professor Serafim Gonçalves was the fattest lawyer in Alagoas—as some affirmed, extending his fatness to the entire state but continuing to limit it to the profession exercised—he was in fact the fattest man in Alagoas.

It was possible that ten or twenty years before, there might have been some citizen still fatter, lawyer or doctor, plantation owner or businessman, but this presumable other had disappeared without leaving even the memory of his name or any particulars about his fatness. And Professor Serafim Gonçalves had confirmed himself before his contemporaries as the fattest lawyer in Maceió—a restrictive way of saying he was the fattest man in the state.

Upon leaving law school in Recife, he hadn't imagined that he would become so fat, despite his family, which he

proudly claimed had the blood of the Dutch invaders, having
produced for generations men who were tall, vigorous, and
even fat (undoubtedly due to the soldiers commanded by
Count Maurice of Nassau in the days when he dreamed of
planting a great empire in the Brazilian Northeast). To these
Dutch ancestors he attributed both the fact that his eyes were
a very light, almost honey-colored, brown, and that his hair
was also brown, with some streaks bordering on blond.

Thus Professor Serafim Gonçalves felt himself tall and
white in a land of brown, swarthy men, half-breeds and
mestizos, not to mention the mulattoes and Negroes. He was
fat, tall, and fair—three things that made him vain.

On that night near the end of the year when, flaunting a
jeweled class ring and sporting a filthy duster which had been
white and beautiful in the morning, he'd leapt from the
Great Western train and received the kisses and embraces of
his parents and family and the congratulations of some
friends who had come to meet him in the station, Professor Serafim Gonçalves was not yet so fat, nor thought
of someday being so. Upon returning to Maceió—which was
not his birthplace because he had been born in Penedo, but
was no less *his* city, to be conquered over the years—he
brought with him the first and most important decision of
his life: to present himself as a candidate for state representative in the next legislature. This would open the way for a
political career which he did not expect to end in the Federal
House of Representatives, or even in the Senate (where he
was sure he would sit someday), but in the Martyrs' Palace,
as governor of the State of Alagoas. Naturally he'd already
established a series of maneuvers in order to attain this ob-
jective, which he didn't consider an ambition, but rather a
right, keeping in mind his special qualifications.

Tall, fat, ruddy, with a splendid belly, he saw himself as
possessing ample credentials to represent, from the physical
point of view, the Alagoan man—a strong man, not frail or

suffering from hookworm. And from the intellectual stand-point, he also judged himself profusely qualified to play such a considerable role in public life. Beside his juridical knowledge, which would surely make him one of the most respected lawyers in Alagoas, he had some literary pretensions. In a student magazine in Recife, he had written two articles, one on the Baron of Penedo—that glory of Alagoas who had wound up as the Brazilian ambassador in London, conversing amicably with Queen Victoria(?)—and another about the Alagoan poet Guimarães Passos, whose mortal remains rested in a Parisian cemetery. During the five years he'd studied in Recife, he had met journalists and writers and one afternoon had drunk beer with a group discoursing on English literature. He had, therefore, practical intellectual experience, and it wasn't completely without reason that in conversations with colleagues and friends in front of Cupertino's bar he often said: "Once, chatting with Gilberto Freyre,* he told me that our patriachal society . . ." And it was enough to cite an opinion from any of the master's works to supply the discussion with the respectable scientific veracity it lacked.

Professor Serafim Gonçalves, remembering those years when he had associated with students and professors—which had caused him to buy a few books and read magazines and newspapers—was overwhelmed by the certainty that these intimacies had guaranteed him a certain private reserve of culture to be used throughout his entire life. And, as he desired to be a politician of intellectual weight, he planned to write a book, which Ramalho House would certainly publish, though it might be better to have it printed by some publisher in the South. Gilberto Freyre, of course, would write the preface. Gonçalves had decided in the beginning that this book—some three hundred pages of strong and

* A famous Brazilian sociologist and leading intellectual figure.

serious prose—would be about the Dutch colonization in Alagoas.

He felt a little Dutch—in the color of his skin, in his honey-colored eyes, in the abundant brown hair shading toward blond—and he suspected that within himself, in the most intimate part of his being, he was sure to encounter a certain vague complicity which would lead him to produce the dreamed of book with reasonable ease. He had more hopes for prominence and public esteem with a book on the Baron of Penedo which he also planned to write, but he stumbled over the difficulty that only in Rio, in the Foreign Office files, could the documentation of the Baron's diplomatic life be found, not to mention the supplemental information which might be at the Brazilian Embassy in London. Moreover, the Dutch element of the first subject was lacking in the Baron of Penedo's existence. With this book on the incursion of the Hollanders into Alagoas—the penetration which had produced his ruddy complexion, his honey-colored eyes and almost blond hair, and which would certainly consecrate him as a magnificent prose stylist—Professor Serafim Gonçalves was sure that he would be elected without difficulties to both the Historical and Geographical Institute of Alagoas (and secretly, he hoped to be received by its president, Orlando Araújo himself) and the Alagoan Academy of Letters. They were the most important honor societies in the state, one in the area of historiography and the other in belles lettres.

Professor Serafim Gonçalves recognized that within him there existed these two directions of the intelligence. Recently graduated and already with several cases in court, he was busy thinking about all these measures essential to his advancement when Getúlio Vargas had closed the Congress and transformed the state governors into federal interventors. In conversations with friends he had cautiously supported the coup d'etat, but he went home disappointed. With the legislative assembly closed, he couldn't run for state representative. Thus there arose a barrier to his dreams. The advisable course would be to attend to the other points of his plan until democratic liberties were restored. He went to bed set on beginning his research on the Dutch influences the following day. He thought about spending a few weeks in Penedo: his birthplace had been the frontier of that New Holland dreamed of by coastal creatures who loved to dwell amidst springs and gardens. He resolved to spend some mornings in the library of the Historical Institute, leafing through old books and moth-eaten documents. But early the next day his clients began bothering him, and there was no time to attend to this. The subsequent days kept him busy, principally a case of separation (motivated by the fact that one of the purest and most religious belles of Alagoan society had contracted a case of gonorrhea which her husband—a debauchee!—had brought home from the brothels) and an appeal to the Supreme Court. Months later, Professor Serafim Gonçalves was convinced that the new regime was only postponing his ambitions. He could put the time to good use, lawyering and making money, which was what he did, and with the greatest boldness. The more he lawyered, the fatter he got. His rolls of fat expanded, not all of them obviously flaccid, some surging forth as an imperious expression of abundance and good health. He got so fat that years later he was considered the fattest lawyer in Maceió—which was the same as asserting that he was the fattest man in the state, for none other could be compared to him. And the fatness, judicious and triumphant, brought him a consideration generally denied to the lean, notable as they might be. When walking down Main Street, the protruding belly captive in a double-breasted coat of white linen, and carrying in a bulging briefcase the renewed proofs of his triumph, he had the sensation that many eyes followed him, envious, admiring, or perhaps merely the dark and bleary eyes of those who see glory and fortune accumulate, capriciously or inexplicably, at the feet of certain mortals. And it wasn't only his imposing physique which, making him stand out from all that undistinguished and insignificant multitude, won him respect. ("I'm not cut from the same cloth," he reflected, in a mute colloquy overflowing with his fervent self-love.) Many considered him the most intelligent man in Alagoas. In the wake of successive courtroom victories, his bons mots spread throughout the bars and registry offices, and were extolled by the loose-tongued groups which, at the doors of shops and around the Official Clock, watched the day pass like a swarm of ants. Then when he was invited by the Bar Association to be included on a triplicate list which would inevitably make him a judge, he refused with a turn of phrase praised by even the Federal Interventor: "Great lawyers don't follow the magistracy." Together with his fatness there also appeared a bad habit. He sniffled. This certainly originated from some deviation of the septum, for one of his nostrils was constantly blocked. He never thought of going to a doctor however, as he considered himself one of the healthiest men in Alagoas.

In this interim there was still another important occurrence in Professor Serafim Gonçalves' life: he married Lígia Tavares, daughter of old Colonel Tavares, plantation owner. Professor Serafim Gonçalves never overcame the conviction that he'd married for love. The young lady, a pale-skinned brunette, neither fat nor thin, had studied in a parochial school, visited Rio, enjoyed the novels of José Lins do Rego and Érico Veríssimo. What's more, he sensed, in a not completely unconscious manner, that when the New State fell and the elections returned, Colonel Tavares wouldn't hesitate to launch him in politics. This would be easy as he had a good electorate, tame and submissive, at his disposal.

Two years after his marriage, Professor Serafim Gonçalves accepted an invitation to teach civil law at the law school in Alagoas; this signified that he would be a full professor when the position became open. So, before turning forty, he was already a respected and worthy person. The students called him Professor. They surrounded him upon leaving class, and he let fall in still tender ears some drops of his steadily increasing life experience. His law office was one of the most prosperous in the state, possibly his fatness inspired confidence and respect in his clients. "A good lawyer should be fat," he was in the habit of pontificating at the door of the Colombo or the Elegant Bar when his friends alluded to the vastness of his paunch. And to himself, he corrected the phrase: a *great* lawyer, for he considered himself the best in the state, the one who most often appealed to the Supreme Court.

When Brazil declared war on Germany—and several of her ships had been sunk by German submarines off coasts quite near to Alagoas—he took advantage of the opportunity to increase his popularity. At the Law School of Alagoas he gave a memorable class, to the extent that, in Maceió, anything could be memorable. He said to the students (and sometimes he liked to repeat, while sitting in the privy or taking a bath, some of the phrases which had been punctuated by vehement hand clapping): "Today I'll not speak to you about ships as mortgageable property. I will speak to you about the Brazilian ships which have been torpedoed by the Germans. I'll speak about the battle of liberty against tyranny, and against the imposition of an ideology based on the falsehood of racial superiority." Deep inside, Professor Serafim Gonçalves felt a little Aryan. By every indication, the Saxon blood of Hitler's soldiers also flowed in his veins, yet this remote Aryanism, certainly mixed with the blood of the Caeté Indians who had so pleasurably eaten Bishop Sardinha and with that of Negroes and Portuguese, did not make his indignation at the traitorous sinking of the ships any less violent and inflamed. Professor Serafim Gonçalves spoke of the drowned bodies which had washed ashore on the anonymous beaches of Sergipe. He liked the expresssion "anonymous beaches" and repeated it. In this lecture he consolidated his prestige as an orator, to such a degree that he became one of the most sought after speakers in the state. He spoke at banquets and ceremonies. Glib-tongued, the words came spontaneously, like the sweat which flowed from his armpits on hot days. Inwardly savoring these provincial oratorical victories, he was carried by his errant imagination to the future awaiting him. He pictured himself, already a senator of the Republic, discoursing in Monroe Palace: "Mr. President, hatred shall not thrive in this country." He saw himself assailing the government's financial policy with a fulgent warning: "The ship of state has already begun to sail the treacherous sea of inflation."

Fat, tall, Flemish in appearance, eyes the color of honey, a first-rate orator, respected professor, promising to one day publish his book on the Dutch influences in Alagoas (and he had not begun this endeavor, which he desired to be voluminous, only for absolute lack of time!), Professor Serafim Gonçalves envisioned himself as a man on the road to a happy future. Strolling through the crooked city streets, hair blowing in the wind, he savored life's pleasures with anticipatory relish. At this time he lived on Peace Avenue, in a palatial house facing the sea. He had installed his office in the anteroom. On very hot days and nights he would open the office's four windows, which looked out on the sea, and passersby could see his law library, one of the best in the state, representing one more factor of security for his clients, who appreciated the diligence and erudition of their defender. What's more, he didn't care for soft covered books. Almost his entire library was leather bound, which seemed to augment the authority of the volumes and conferred on the shelves an air of inarguable nobility.

It happened that, in this period, he started going bald. His head of hair, perhaps the handsomest in the state with its thick, light brown locks, was being slowly and implacably diminished by time. But, even going bald, he was still shaggy-haired, as if the remaining locks persisted in hiding the pitiless disappearance of the hundreds or perhaps thousands of hairs which were vanishing day by day. Professor Serafim Gonçalves mused that baldness was not undesirable in a public figure, as if it evoked nights of study and meditation consulting works of jurisprudence. And while his hairline retreated surreptitiously, Professor Serafim Gonçalves, lulled by ambition, confided to himself that his life was almost complete. The future held good pickings in store. He need only await the country's return to democracy, which would inevitably occur after the war, to begin his political career. It was no longer a secret to anyone that he would begin as a federal representative; there even existed the possibility of his being one of the opposition candidates for senator. Though maintaining good relations with the Federal Interventor, Professor Serafim Gonçalves did not admit the possibility of serving on the side of the government if the occasion should arise. He felt that, to further his ambitions, there was nothing better than the opposition banner, which would permit him to give free rein to his concept of himself as an orator. And, while the New State lasted, despite some periodic rumors that day by day Vargas was making greater concessions to the armed forces in order to stay in power, Professor Serafim Gonçalves lived in arduous expectation. It was as if his true existence were going to begin only on the day he managed to get his fingers in the public pie.

During this period there was still another change in his life: he developed a taste for cognac. At first, he drank only a glass a day, to whet his appetite before lunch. Afterwards, he began to increase the dosage and incorporated cognac into his life, which caused him a slight euphoria. Though he realized that this love of drink constituted a tiny weakness or personal aberration, he did not consider it detrimental to his ambitions. He drank cognac the way his friends drank beer at the Colombo Bar or played poker in the rear of the Commercial Billiards. He didn't think, therefore, that the habit

possessed any censurable aspect. A singular preference, it
contributed even more to personalizing him. Carried away
by his dream and believing in it, he exultantly heard imaginary voices. It was in the Martyrs' Palace and a cabinet
official was saying: "Representative Cansanção has brought
a case of cognac from Europe for the Governor." He was
the Governor, and as quickly changed into a senator and,
standing in a corridor of the Monroe Palace, listened as if he
were invisible to a veteran political reporter informing a
young cub: "He is a true gentleman and statesman. A man
of great culture, author of a book on the Dutch colonization
in the Northeast and a biography of the Baron of Penedo,
an exemplary work, greatly praised by the critics. A stupen-
dous orator, and also very refined, a connoisseur of European
cognacs."

Sometimes, however, Professor Serafim Gonçalves would
go overboard. Thus it happened one morning when, seated
at a table in the Colombo Bar, he learned that Alexandre
Viana had committed suicide. Alexandre had not been a
friend of his, only a nodding acquaintance and the son of a
man he had admired. Still, it was a suicide, a terrible act.
Professor Serafim Gonçalves judged the first morning cognac
to be insufficient. He ordered another and, while waiting
for the waiter to come back, drummed his fingers distractedly
on the marble tabletop. His companion was telling a story
about a fox which, that very morning, had been clubbed to
death in the city center, near Martyrs' Square.

"Imagine, a fox in the heart of the city," he remarked.

But the exclamation disguised the tenuous interest the
story held for him. He couldn't understand Alexandre
Viana's suicide, and the speaker was ignorant of the motives.
It was known (it was public and notorious) that the suicide
had had a protégée—a euphemistic way of saying that he had
maintained two homes. A year before he had taken up with
a girl who worked in Customs or the Excise Office or in one

of the social welfare institutions. Was it possible that Alexandre Viana had had his hand in the till? Everything was hypothetical, but the truth was bound to come to light shortly. In Alagoas, only the treasures hidden by the Dutch were never discovered. Everything else was known, whether the name of a lottery winner or a case of incest.

"Did he leave a letter?"

The other knew nothing for the time being. And chewing softly on some remnant of food, he half showed his discolored gums. His mouth looked like a chicken's asshole.

Eyeing with secret resentment the portrait of Getúlio Vargas hanging on the wall, Professor Serafim Gonçalves took his third cognac at the counter. It was exactly time to give his class at the university. He would go to the burial.

"The body is still in the mortuary. I just now met Doctor Lages, the coroner."

"They're talking about embezzlement, but I don't believe it."

A light stench of garbage hung in the air—that age-old sordid stench which the sea wind could never extinguish, for all that it might blow.

"Maceió doesn't even respect the dead. There are some who are going around spreading the rumor that he was assassinated by the Brotherhood."

As the sun rose higher, the number of beggars increased. The strong sun attracted them.

"A lot of typhoid cases, I heard today."

A nasal voice: "This will only come to an end the day they chlorinate Maceió's drinking water."

A man, blind and pockmarked, accompanied by a child with a harmonica, stretched out his hand to Professor Serafim Gonçalves.

"They're saying that a German submarine sank another Brazilian ship."

"Me, if I were the government, I'd have them round up

all the Integralists.* They're the ones who tell the Germans where the ships are."

Thus spoke an accountant who, months before, had been taken to police headquarters. There they had given him two dozen strokes on the palms of his hands on account of the advanced ideas he was spreading around the bars in conversations with friends and acquaintances. And as if his hands still burned, he reiterated, full of civic indignation: "They're the ones."

A bell clanged hoarsely in the Church of Our Lady of Redemption. In a tavern, a salesclerk wearing suspenders was drinking sugarcane juice. The streetcars screeched gratingly on their tracks. A justice official was bragging in the doorway of a notary public. As Professor Serafim Gonçalves turned the corner, a yellowed hand stretched toward him:

"Young man, alms for the poor."

Climbing the first steps of the building which some stubborn Alagoans had managed to construct in order to disseminate the principles of Law and Justice among their fellow citizens, Serafim Gonçalves turned his head. A blond sailor was passing by on the sidewalk. He stopped to watch him, and later could not have said how long the contemplation had lasted. A pupil yanked him from the inadmissible daydream.

"There's an American warship in the harbor."

During the entire class Professor Serafim Gonçalves appeared distracted. The words refused to come. His troubled thoughts followed the unknown sailor who, coming from distant lands, had crossed his path, disturbing him.

---

* Brazilian political party sympathetic to the Fascist cause during World War II.

THE STAIRWAY

Alexandre Viana committed suicide around three o'clock in the morning. About two hours later, on Belleview Street, some men brandishing clubs would bring down the fox.

He died without seeing the fox which, since early in the morning, had been wandering about the city's center. Naturally he couldn't have seen her at the moment she paused close by his house to drink water from a tiny puddle for the simple reason that he wasn't there. Alexandre Viana hadn't slept at home nor, to tell the truth, even slept.

He could have run into the fox moments before when she, passing near the cargo warehouses in Jaraguá, had stopped in the vicinity of the Western Telegraph Agency—as if her sharp wild animal ears could capture the ciphered code which came silently from the sea by way of submarine cables. But it so happened that when Alexandre Viana, coming from Enaura's house, turned the corner and the pressure of the sea wind became stronger on his face, the fox, moved by a sudden impulse of speed, had practically begun to run, and would shortly reach the first of the four windows of Professor

23

Serafim Gonçalves' house. In the distance she lost her original form and substance and was transformed into a dog. And it wasn't likely that Alexandre Viana would have had his attention drawn by the skulking shadow of a dog becoming lost at the end of a poorly illuminated street.

Anyway, Alexandre Viana didn't see the fox. And strangely enough, at the instant he turned the corner and raised his eyes to look at the thick livid walls of the storage depots which, in the silence violated only by brief, delicate, unplaceable rustles, expelled an odor close to that of an immense block of brown sugar being irremediably dissolved in the shadow, Alexandre was thinking precisely of animals. A scene from his childhood had come to his mind—not one of those forgotten episodes which only an aroma or a sound manage to resuscitate, hoisting it into the memory like an old banner damaged in an ancient catastrophe, but an image which had accompanied him throughout his life and which used to awaken him like the persistent metallic cadence of a hammer.

Alexandre Viana had just enrolled in the parochial high school on the afternoon he went to the square in front of the jail to see the new circus. He bought a piece of peeled sugarcane and slowly moved closer. Already the great center post was set and all about there was a hurry-scurry nourished by din and disorder: and within this there vibrated the principle of profound order by which circuses rise up, suddenly, in any square, to the sound of the music which attracts children and pacifies the animals. Moved by a curiosity mixed with timidity and apprehension, Alexandre Viana approached the cages and stalls where the animals were imprisoned and contemplated, not without a certain repugnance, an old and stinking lion whose filthy snout moved from right to left, attempting to frighten off a cloud of flies. There was also a bony tiger which examined everyone sideways, with its hard and bloodstained eyes promising vengeance—an impossible vengeance, set in some frigid territory the other side of time and death.

Further along, an earth-colored elephant trampled the ground—and was at the same time a comic and respectable figure in its claylike rotundity. Yet, it wasn't at the elephant, which appeared almost a free animal, given its surprising proportions, that Alexandre Viana directed his gaze. He felt somehow fascinated by the two outraged creatures, the lion and the tiger, prisoners in stinking parallel cages. In the stare of both the beasts he read a tremendous hatred of slavery, a horror going beyond the frontiers of any irrationality to be affirmed, in all its vehemence, by their interminable attempts to flee the iron bars. In that moment, Alexandre Viana felt himself stunned by the nauseating dirty atmosphere of terror emanating from the cages. Both the lion and tiger were condemned until the coming of death, a death springing from captivity itself or from old age. They would never escape—they couldn't even kill themselves, nor did they even know the significance of this ultimate act.

In the waning afternoon Alexandre Viana returned home, thinking about creatures which could escape from slavery, flee the cage, they themselves being the authors of their own liberation. The following day, he asked Father Sizenando why irrational animals didn't commit suicide, and the answer coincided with what, intimately, he'd already known. He entered the classroom with the overwhelming sensation that only man, a rational animal, the only one which had been promised paradise, could sacrifice himself. The tigers, lions, and elephants were terrestrial animals. No god had promised them a paradise. Not having the right to an inferno which could consume them eternally, they were barred from self-slaughter. For them, life wasn't a simple waiting room for eternity, a place of passage spanning the rushing ocean, where one breathed the odor of sacks of sugar heaped up in stores and warehouses. It was their own animal eternity, and at most they could, if they had had the gift of recollection, evoke those early times in the forests and mountains, in an earthly paradise from whence they'd been taken by the cunning of hunters of wild beasts.

From that day on, Alexandre Viana began to keep in his consciousness the secret of his eventual liberation. Life was a cage. The very universe, with its innumerable galaxies, its days and nights, its star systems ruled by a fundamental harmony and the weight of their myths, was also a cage. But, in this prison, whether metaphysical or visible in the four walls of a cell or in twisted city streets, there was a captive with the power to escape at any moment. Since that instant of discovery, Alexandre began to accept suicide as a kind of emergency exit. Periodically, the recollection of that childhood afternoon when he'd seen the circus go up returned to his memory, and with it the image of an animal capable of escaping from its cage, an animal author of its own death and trained to thus construct its own eternity.

After leaving high school, Alexandre Viana didn't accept the advice of his father, who wanted him to be a lawyer. He preferred going into business for himself—insurance brokerage, irregular transactions born from conversations around the Official Clock with friends and acquaintances who had distributorships. Years later, he was manager of the local airline agency (and sometimes, it occurred to him that airplanes had an emergency exit which could also be used during the flight, while airborne, and that it must surely afford the chance user a dizzy sensation of escape and liberty, a kind of reverse resurrection in irreversibly blue space).

He married a girl who, so to speak, had been his childhood sweetheart. And he'd had the clear awareness that he was finally caged on the very night of his wedding, that wedding without a honeymoon, for they hadn't gone anywhere, and were sleeping together for the first time in the cramped bedroom of the house he'd rented in Wide Point (and Alexandre

Viana remembered that, at the very moment he'd lain upon Alice's body and felt her tremble like a bird in the darkness, he'd heard a freight train's whistle furrow the night's emptiness). The cage had stopped being an atmosphere—as was the case of the the city where idle men went to and fro, pausing to buy a box of matches or get a shoeshine, eye the crease of their khaki trousers or confide the latest gossip or slander to an acquaintance, tearing down reputations—to take on a disturbing materiality. He was like the criminal who only feels himself truly imprisoned when the cell's iron door closes behind him, and who had judged himself free when, with handcuffs on, he walked through the streets full of sun and sounds. On that nuptial night, when Alice, wearing a cambric nightgown, furtively left the room, and he heard the distant slam of the bathroom door, Alexandre Viana considered himself captured. Invisible hunters had reached his forests and mountains, and he sensed himself snared or fallen into a trap.

His life continued placidly in that house of narrow rooms. The living room full of trinkets—for Alice's obsession was to collect the most grotesque ceramic ornaments possible—seemed more cramped everyday, especially after two colored portraits of his wife's parents, presenting images of them both still young and momentarily reverential, had been hung on the walls, or perhaps after some horrendous artificial flowers had filled a green jar placed on a rosewood coffee table. And the days passed, days of sand and wind, refreshing days of nothing, and the conviction assailed Alexandre that he, in his words and routine, was pretending to be alive.

Their first child was born, and Alice, after months of dizziness and vomit, discovered in this tiny creature, weak and subject to the runs, a better reason to live than the artificial flowers and the comic porcelain objects.

Alexandre Viana observed that the child separated them, seemed to make them freer, eliminated their excessive togetherness, assured each one a zone of shadow and secrecy which was mistaken for contemplation and propriety. And for years they both lived separated by a mutual reserve, as if they didn't dare to confide their secrets and meditations to one another. Until, one evening, a girl had entered the agency and headed toward Alexandre Viana, who was at the counter dealing with the shipping of a few boxes of pharmaceutical products. She wanted a ticket to Recife. It was her second trip to the agency. All the available tickets had been sold so she was relying on the possibility of a cancellation. This time, Alexandre Viana waited on her. He learned that she wanted to go to a brother's wedding. He also learned that she had gone to the movies the day before, and her tanned face testified to her presence at the beach the past Sunday. The following day in the morning, Alexandre Viana managed to arrange a ticket, even giving her a discount. She welcomed this help with an absurd display of gratitude which illuminated her black eyes.

A week later she appeared again in the agency, wearing a yellow organdy dress with a daring neckline. Alexandre saw her from the rear of the office and approached the counter. She gave him a key ring she'd brought from Recife. Her name was Enaura, and she wasn't in the least bothered by his wedding ring. She was evidently no longer a virgin. She'd given herself to a soldier in Recife, two years before, and she admitted that she'd had a few other affairs.

Alice didn't need to make a great effort to perceive the presence of another woman in Alexandre's life. The excuses that he was working overtime at the office, the Sundays away from home on the pretext that he was accompanying a company inspector who wanted to visit the towns of Deodoro and Sweet Creek, all this circumstantial evidence accumulated in her spirit. Her husband no longer sought her at night, alleging that he was dead tired; and a few confidences from friends took care of the rest. Without recriminations, she sealed herself in a chaste expectancy. She couldn't explain why she kept, beneath the pink paper of the tiny oratory resting on her bedroom bureau, the blue envelope with the anonymous letter telling of her husband's disgusting affair with some Enaura. It was a piece of common typing paper, on which a faceless informant had written in fine letters seeking to imitate newsprint: *Your husband has taken a tramp named Enaura for a mistress, and has furnished a house for her in Jaraguá.* Below, it was signed: *A friend.* This anonymous letter had been mentally written late one afternoon, in a big warehouse smelling of sugar and textile fibers. He'd thought of calling Enaura a bitch (and in truth he considered her one), but finally desisted, preferring a more respectful term as the intended recipient was a married woman.

While he slowly wrote the letters, as if he were designing them, the man who'd sent it had sensed the heavy gray smell of the evening entering his nostrils—a smell of ships, of rusty scrap iron, of dark closed sheds where foodstuffs destined for shipping piled up, of greenish, gelatinous residues spewed up on the beaches, of salt brine imperceptibly covering the fronts of buildings like a transparent marine patina. But sometimes, it was as if the sea did not exist, and he lived among stones, in a nest of snakes. And his letter contained an untruth or an error. Alexandre Viana hadn't furnished a house for Enaura. She'd moved to Jaraguá from Farol with an old aunt who for many years had carried on an affair with a sergeant of the Military Police, a half-breed named Cajueiro. It was one of those cases which, so long prolonged, finally takes on a platonic aura, so that it wasn't every week that the sergeant took off his lustrous soldier's boots in the bedroom where there was a lithograph of Saint Judas Tadeu, the saint of impossible losses. The aunt was also her counselor. She didn't condemn Enaura's relationship, not only because she perhaps nurtured the conviction that every woman needs a man, but also because she possessed blind and foolish confidence in her niece, thinking it possible that she would some day take Alexandre Viana away from his legitimate spouse. She was certain Enaura would achieve this in the end, giving to her liason the majestic dignity of marriage. In Maceió, such cases were common.

The move to Jaraguá had been motivated by the fact that Enaura didn't want any new whisperings in reference to her home in the old neighborhood, where the sergeant had already been seen coming and going almost every day.

Alexandre Viana had countersigned the rental contract for the new house. Besides a few small expenses he'd financed only one piece of furniture: a double bed, purchased at Ladoski's, which Enaura had accepted a little bashfully, on the pretense that it was a present. Since Enaura worked, she turned out to be inexpensive and counted for little in his budget. The author of the anonymous letter wasn't unaware of these facts and, upon writing the accusation, had had to admit he was embroidering a bit, augmenting the information with false data. And, shaping the final letters of his missive, he imagined the moment in which the recipient, opening the blue envelope, would try to guess if the sender were a man or a woman. For a few minutes, he mulled over the mystery of an enigmatic and ambiguous signature, surrounded by an invisible fringe of sarcasm.

Alice had kept the letter in the blue envelope, hidden it beneath the saints, and listened to the advice of older people who persuaded her to bear those days of bitterness. The nights Alexandre Viana didn't sleep at home became a part of her life's routine. He didn't need to allude to occasional overtime work at the agency. If he hadn't arrived home by eight at night, it was more than certain that he wasn't going to come. She would put the child to bed, eat dinner in silence, lean out the sitting room window for a few moments, and time would pass: a rococo time in which her trinkets were transformed into fragile monuments of a silent yellow world, sustained by its own lack of hope and massive adherence to routine.

Alice knew there was nothing more to hope for, only to live among knickknacks which would never dissolve and would endure, with their bizarre crockery passivity, whatever outrage of time. Life between her and Alexandre went by in a ridiculous purgatory of appearances, in which a zone of silence (as if the reserve of both were suddenly invoked) determined the flow of prohibitions. Both grew silent, not daring to exceed the limits of the tiny, repeated domestic ceremonies: the grocery bills, the money so she could visit the shops in the afternoon, buying clothes and some toy for Otávio, the conversations so empty of meaning it was amazing that the words, with their cutting edge of significance, could arrange the two of them about the table or in the sitting room.

To flee that emptiness—so great one could hear the singing of the neighbor's canary or a footstool scraping on the sidewalk in front of the corner grocery—Alexandre would run to Enaura's house and drag her to the bedroom. There, united with her nakedness, stroking the vaccination mark on her thigh, impetuously touching the black pubic hairs which contrasted with his light brown locks, immobilized before the animal verity of her body, he attained peace. She received his caresses without reciprocating with any initiative, merely waiting (after all, he hadn't even removed his tie, remaining dressed except for his jacket). Without articulating the briefest word, he suddenly felt himself exist and endure in the irreversible void of the universe. Yes, he was in the cage, with the female who would never satiate his cold desire for liberty, his thirst for escape which he cast forth in the silence of the starry night for the consideration of the gods, wherever they might be. It hadn't been enough that these gods, hidden in the highest galaxies, fixing mankind

with their thousand supercelestial eyes, had invented the
flesh. It was beyond the flesh that Alexandre Viana turned
and found nothing, as if something had been concealed,
transforming his search into disappointment. Only Enaura's
gesture, seeking him with her hand in the first movement
of a brief and dirty ballet, unbuttoning his fly and turning
her torso (and Alexandre Viana's gaze rested on the wrinkled
aureoles of her breasts, which accompanied the slow flexing
of her upper body), jerked him from his dumb silence, leading him to free himself of his garments and stanch the
thoughts which gushed from his head in a clear and perfect
torrent. Only her gesture, lucidly relieving his desperation,
opened on his horizon of dumb silence and tedium a clearing of reflection which illuminated him with its bright sharp
light. Like an animal which escapes and, after a few seconds
of bewilderment, returns again to captivity, so he felt when
his desire changed to wheezing pacification, and for a few
minutes he let himself remain stretched out in bed, sealed
by the vacuum of an ephemeral and summerlike hypnosis.
He was cornered again—the door he had thought he'd found
in the second when, squeezing Enaura's buttocks and resting
his head on her shoulder, he had attained his spasm, had
faded and lost any imaginable consistency. It was a door of
nothing in the night of nothing. In that fragile moment
nothing existed but the brief and panting conjugation of two
desires shuffled together and finally dissipated. Above the
roof beams and tiles of the house flew fragments of the great
wind which, having come from far away regions where the
days are eternally cold and white, had gradually lost its polar
consistency. It had turned ardent and profuse, its hot breath
stirring the fronds of coconut palms and carrying the aroma
of guava trees in bloom. Alexandre observed that Enaura
was referring to the gale (or a broken tile) and her phrase,
lost in the space filled by the uninterrupted rustling of the

breeze, only now returned to his notice, as if the wind had carried it to farms where fat mangaba trees quivered like grave matrons disturbed, and had then returned it to him, available and intact. The sententious and banal nature of the phrase followed him like a furtive dog, or even like a fox skulking in the shadows. And thus he slept: the wind the wind the wind. He didn't repeat the words but, as his eyelids became heavier, he saw himself pursued by their silly reiteration. The wind didn't appear subject to any meteorlogical rule or law. Its chill changed to sultriness, and even within its fiery tropical warmth it held a smattering of moisture, and it soothed him so that he slept with his arms crossed on his chest, like the dead.

Alexandre Viana couldn't have said how many times, behind the bars of his cage, he'd heard the wind blow in the sonorous and empty night. And he wasn't interested in knowing on how many occasions his eyes had rested on the vaccination mark on Enaura's thigh. The morning after, he'd drink the coffee that Enaura, dressed in a gaudy bathrobe (which inexplicably made her look like a whore he had met on Hay Street, years before), always made, and leave for work, governed by an abrupt haste which hid his desire to be alone for a few minutes during the streetcar ride. Upon reaching the beach, he would contemplate the ships, one or two docked, others anchored in the bay, as if they awaited nothing and their temporary repose in the vicinity of the moorage were an incorruptible permanency. At the agency, he'd be enveloped by the bureaucracy of diminutive departures—tickets to Recife, João Pessoa, Natal, Fortaleza, Teresina, Belém, Manaus, tickets to Aracaju, Bahia, Canavieiras, Vitória do Espírito Santo, Rio.

"But is it necessary to change planes?"

"How many kilos of luggage may I take?"

"If it weren't for the war, I'd go by boat."

"I heard that a German sub sank another Ita."

"But they told me there was going to be a new bus line between Maceió and Rio."

Men wanted to travel, for business, for hospital internment, an appointment—and they argued over days, hours of departure and arrival, transport to the airport, weight of the luggage. And women also wanted to travel, to a wedding, a baptism, a visit to a relative. The most varied pretexts cropped up while they were examining the flight schedules. They were astounded by the new increase in ticket prices, assumed serious expressions upon hearing the commentary of a salesman from São Paulo insinuating a relationship between the price of air fares and the exchange rate of the dollar.

"And my invoice, where's my invoice?"

"Have you gotten the confirmation yet?"

"So I'll reserve the seat and come to pay tomorrow."

There was merchandise to expedite. It was necessary to go to the airport, but the truck still hadn't come back from the gas station where it was being greased. One of the company's planes was being held up in Salvador, waiting for a part which hadn't yet come from Rio. The wife of a chief justice had sent to ask if he couldn't arrange a few newspapers from Rio for her. A character with a hoarse voice left the counter after they'd assured him that the medicine someone in the South had sent him hadn't arrived. Alexandre Viana gave orders, answered the telephone, pointed to a packing crate by the stairs leading to his second floor office, lit a cigarette. And the spongy hours passed, sucking up all that was fluid in time, like words and water.

Alexandre Viana often went out for a little while on the pretext that he needed a shoeshine and a pack of cigarettes. He'd cross the street which widened until reaching the Official Clock and there divided. Sitting in the shoeshine boy's chair, he'd hear Gonguila tell him how much money the

Knights of the Hills would need for the next Carnival; or perhaps he'd hear nothing, only letting the bootblack talk while his eyes followed Ramona, the city's most famous pederast, down the other side of the street. Ramona was advancing towards the Helvética, from which there came the murmur of laughter loosed around a table full of empty beer bottles. The passing streetcar hid him from view. He sported, despite the heat, a worn cashmere suit that certainly had not been tailored for him. He had received it already worn and indefinite in color, as if it had borne for years the routine vehemence of the rains in cold climes. On the other side of the wall was Zanotti's bar. A man lit a cigarette using a burning cord which swung in the air—its end was a smoldering eye—another swallowed a refreshment made from a greenish liquid and grated ice. He stepped down from the chair, let a bill flutter down among the cans of wax (Gonguila, head inclined over the drawer where he was putting the chocolate colored rag used to give luster to the shoes, had stopped looking at him), and left, crossing the paths of people who came and went, almost trampling or crushing a beggar who, with twisted hands and feet, was dragging himself along the sidewalk, and whose head didn't even reach the knees of the passing adults. Further along, he stopped by a group in which men wearing tropical cotton, khaki, and linen predominated. He listened to their chatter for a few minutes, sniffed out the shredding of lives and reputations, the unravelling of shabby tricks and commonplaces. It was the city's latest scandal, the story of a man who, arriving home unexpectedly, had surprised his wife in bed with a government pest exterminator; he'd killed her with two shots, but her lover had managed to flee in his shorts, leaping a wall and leaving his uniform on a chair in the violated bedroom.

Sometimes, the placid indolence of those prattling groups scattered about the Official Clock while the afternoon flowed by was conspiratorially unsettled by the sudden crash of a shot. One of the men in white would fall dead—and the afternoon would continue, flexible as a bow.

With frightened eyes, very short hair, and an air of innocence and stupor on his colorless face which seemed to avoid the sun and the wind, Guabiraba approached the chattering group, enveloping it with a soft gesture. Perhaps he came only to hustle some spare change, or to hear the end of the story about the government exterminator. Alexandre Viana said good-bye and wandered at random. Carnival music came from a shoestore which was going out of business. Some people were stationed by the door of the Commercial Billiards, conversing.

At dusk, it could be said that the city conversed deaths, adulteries, illnesses, and drinking sprees. It mounted discussions on politics or the result of the numbers lottery. Someone was saying that the evening before he'd run into a cheap whore near Martyrs' Square, had taken her to the Blindman's Baths, and there possessed her on a hard plank which was less an improvised bed than a table; another was speaking of a binge which had terminated with a swim at night in the Catolé (everyone had ended up naked, men and women, and thanks to the alcoholic euphoria it was as if they were in a kind of licentious earthly paradise); a third guaranteed that he'd seen, days before, a doctor's wife heading toward a new trysting place that had opened in the Well; another swore his neighbor was a queer (and the man from behind the counter was in one of the groups, silently drinking in every word as if it were a delicate, everlasting froth, collecting information for the anonymous letters which, at least once a week, he produced in his room in the Old Palace).

Urchins made sport of Guabiraba, mocking his too short pants and haircut.

So Alexandre Viana would return to the agency, begin to examine invoices and dispatches, make recommendations about certain containers. Night having fallen, he'd roll down his shirt sleeves, tighten the knot of his tie, put on his suit coat, and depending on the day of the week, his mood, whatever fortuitous fact, set a course for the house where Alice moved among porcelain bric-a-brac, or to the room where Enaura awaited him wearing a wine-colored bathrobe. And once again Alexandre Viana would remember the woman from Hay Street; it could be said that she wore her peignoir as if she carried a light and supple treasure which made her comparable to certain women of high society, women who moved vaporously in the morning's crystalline center after nights when, in dark hermetic rooms, they had let themselves be loved without permitting their husbands the vision of their bodies, bodies which reserve seemed to turn momentarily immaculate when touched by almost convulsive hands.

Trinkets. Peignoir. Trinkets. The portrait of Getúlio Vargas on the wall. The noise of motorcycles. The wind. The shadow of the warehouse. The noseless beggar who had asked him for alms. The stamp, violated by the postmark, on an envelope in the bureau. The blue checkered tablecloth on the table where there were only two plates—Enaura's aunt had gone out to visit an old woman in Combona and hadn't come back yet. And so it was, and so it would be forever.

But there came a night when Alexandre Viana left Enaura's house as dawn was beginning to rise in the dark gray sky where the stars were imperceptibly changing position. He didn't see the fox even when, after crossing the bridge over Salt Creek, his eyes rested on the deserted square and the building of the Northeastern Brazil Power and Light Company. He walked, pursued by the trailing wind which cooled his legs, crossed the railroad tracks, climbed the hillside beside the cathedral, came to the sidewalk in front of the Excise Office, and further along, before the end of the square and near the Old Palace, crossed over to the left-hand

side. He opened the door to the agency, leaving it ajar behind him, turned on the light and climbed the stairs leading
to the second floor.

Alexandre Viana arrived at the agency around two in the
morning, at least Enaura declared to the police that he'd
left her house at one thirty and he'd certainly spent half an
hour on the way. For an hour he rummaged through papers
so that at the first examination it would be evident that he'd
left the agency in order, and any shameful, defamatory hypothesis would be eliminated. He'd already decided not to
write a letter or a note, and he wanted any superficial or
rapid investigation to show the truth, that the agency's ac-
counts were up to date. There had been no slipup or embezzlement, and he was leaving everything in order. This
thought occurred suddenly to Alexandre Viana, who was
now seeing a profound order springing from the sinuous disorder of his life and from existence in general. It was as if
the world were a little table where a group of trinkets were
arranged, and the randomness of this arrangement had been
converted, by some invisible harmony or usage into a manifest order repelling any modification or violation. He opened
the last drawer, and within there was only one object: the
pistol he'd bought years before and never used. His gaze
rested on the stairway handrail. He would never climb those
steps again. On the table there was a bundle of newspapers
from Rio—they were the newspapers he'd promised the Chief
Justice's wife. He stared at them with a sensation of disappointment, almost of rage. He'd told the messenger to take
them to the Chief Justice's house the night before, certainly
he'd forgotten. But everything else was in its place—Enaura's
peignoir was hanging behind her bedroom door, Alice's
trinkets lay, brilliant and blind as treasures, in the stifling
sitting room. His son slept. Alexandre Viana gave a start. He
hoped the child would one day understand why he'd resolved
not to remain in his life, watching him grow until they went

their separate ways and became taciturn strangers. For certainly there would come an hour when the child, having become a youth or a grown man would risk, in the depths of his consciousness, a question: "Why?" And Alexandre Viana wouldn't be there to assure him that he had behaved as he did exactly because of the nonexistence of this *why* emitted by the living, dumbly articulated by those who had not yet died. The postmark on the stamp was contracting like a pupil in the sun. The trinket. The ship. The peignoir. The shined shoes. The whispering wind, raising sand and sprinkling leaves from cashew trees. The rotting ships in the mangrove pools. The flies carrying typhoid. The tiger's breath. The lion's bloody eyes. Enaura's pubic hair. All the doors were closing in the mist. The wind no longer carried the fragrance of guava trees more aromatic than the ocean. The people themselves, despoiled of what was human within them, became words and congested his mind. It was raining—it was a rain of words. The wind blew—it was a wind of words. The world wasn't made of skies, clouds, cities, sugarcane mills, ports, dams, yards, old cars, streets, power plants, houses, men. It was made only and exclusively of words— and the people spoke in words. Even the paving stones of Maceió were made of words. Alexandre Viana ate words, slept words, worked words. And he felt more alone than ever, as if the very weapon which sketched itself before his eyes would turn into a word. Rio. Canavieiras. Ilhéus. Salvador. Aracaju. Recife. João Pessoa.

"A German submarine sank another one of Lloyd's ships."

"They told me it was one of the Costeira Line's."

"Will I change planes in Salvador or go straight through?"

Alexandre Viana raised the pistol, his finger found the trigger; his entire body felt the metallic coldness of the barrel—it was the same sensation as when, with head lowered and feet up, he was in the dentist's chair having a root canal done. Then the shot reverberated, with a sudden uproar,

dry and resplendent as an earthquake, as if the earth, once
compact and impenetrable, had cracked down to its fiery
core. And fusing with the explosion which contaminated the
immense lunar night, a light, perhaps the swinging second
story lamp, perhaps the obfuscation of a star's light. Was
there still a stairway—for whom to climb? For whom to
descend? Alexandre Viana never knew, because precisely at
that moment he ceased to exist, he moved no more in the
world's dry and opaque desolation. For an infinitesimal
moment, while the sea resounded, Alexandre had the sensation he was not living. He only dreamed. He was dreaming
his own reality. And nothing would happen, for it was a
dream, the virginal foam of a dream which enveloped him
like a spiral staircase envelops the lighthouse keeper's steps
at nightfall. With a vertiginous transposition (as in his
adolescent days when, hardly having closed his eyes to sleep,
he dreamed he was falling, and didn't know that this imaginary fall was the announcement of his virility) he saw himself as if he were being dreamed. Yes, he was being dreamed,
he didn't exist—and death, even deliberate and sought by
his own hands, would signify only the end of the dream, the
same as when, an adolescent, it was enough to open his eyes
to verify that he'd ceased falling, and the afflictive fall which
was carrying him to his first orgasm was nothing more than
a dream.

As soon as the bell rang, he descended, running, the high
school stairs. He wanted to be on time for the circus matinee.
His hand had let go of the handrail, he'd tripped between
two steps, had fallen. And now, perhaps in a now outside
time or space, or similar to the margin between the dock
and a ship's hull, between the thunder and incandescence,
the wind and the broken roof tile, the bathrobe and the
trinket, the air ticket and the cage, between the packing box
on which the warning "Fragile, Glassware" was tacked and
the interrogation which fifteen years later would come from

the throat of a young man, between the statue of a statesman fading in the shadow when he had crossed the square an hour before and the key he'd put in his pocket upon leaving the door to the agency ajar—and again between the report and the resplendency, the bathrobe and the trinket, the cage and the wind, inside death hard as a diamond, Alexandre Viana saw a stairway. But *his* death—a personal episode or happening, like a birthday, the taste of a cup of coffee drunk standing, the impatient movement of a hand clutching at a naked breast beneath a sheet—was like the sea wind or the whistling of a ship. It came to him from without, forged by an exterior reality which dissipated in immateriality and abstraction and, an invading dream, occupied him like an intruder in that spasmodic instant in which he divested himself of his life like someone undressing for bed, conceding the grotesque or torpid spectacle of his forever offended nudity to the absolute emptiness located beyond the constellations and the flow of time, time which, guarding life and movement, memory and ecstasy, was also the faithful depository of death and decomposition.

THE BATHROBE

So, they killed the fox . . ."
The woman was lying in one of the wards of the hospital where she'd been admitted as a charity case. She'd arranged herself so as to keep her head high up on the folded pillow. Dressed in a wine-colored bathrobe, she was listening to the story being narrated by the patient on her left, a lean woman who bore tiny black spots on her face, neck, and arms (and certainly on the rest of her body, concealed by a dirty gown, as well). It was the story of a fox, killed that morning in the city's center.

The bathrobe the woman wore had been given to her in Penedo by a traveling salesman, and since then she'd never been separated from it. In the house on Hay Street, where she'd gone upon arriving in Maceió, she'd used it daily with the unfounded but vehemently held belief that it gave her a certain social status. She imagined that the fine ladies who lived in the beautiful houses in Farol and Pajuçara, and who sometimes stepped down from cars in front of the shops on Main Street, possessed identical bathrobes.

There was a male nurse in the hospital, well, not exactly

a nurse, but a janitor who months before had been suddenly promoted from sweeping the hospital floors. He had so often watched the real nurse, another former janitor, that he had learned how to boil a syringe, cut open an ampul, and force the needle into the scant and wrinkled flesh of the diseased. That morning when he had come to give her a shot, he had told her that a man had committed suicide and that the body had already been taken to the mortuary. He had volunteered the information while massaging the muscle of her right arm, after the injection.

"He killed himself with one shot. But some say he was assassinated by the Brotherhood."

And he added, putting the needle away in its black case, "Murdered."

In her head the two stories became mixed, that of the fox being bludgeoned to death and that of the man who'd committed suicide or been murdered: The Brotherhood . . . Many times she'd heard tell of those men paid to kill—who vanished after the crime, sent to Goiás and other ends of the earth, who disappeared from jail when caught, were absolved by the jury or appeared in turn slaughtered, their livid chops sealed by silence.

The woman had been admitted to treat a case of the clap and a soft chancre. In reality, it was as if she were rotten. At least, in one of those discussions so common in charity wards, a companion, a scrofulous and irritable creature who had been released days later, had accused her of being rotten with her worldly diseases. She'd retorted with another insult in which she'd insinuated that the other had leprosy; but by evening they'd already made peace and were talking together like good friends. Her treatment was given in a series, designed to cure her syphilis since, though she continued to douche, the gonorrhea and the soft chancre were already practically cured. At least she'd stopped feeling pain and burning when she urinated. She received an injection every

day, and at the instant the needle penetrated her muscle the
nurse always said something to her—he told her that the
new surgeon had bought a car and parked it on the other
side of the hospital, that the child with typhoid fever had
died, that the old lady from Anadia—the one with swollen
eyes—was very ill and that the wife of the short egg salesman,
who had come from São Miguel dos Campos (or was it
Quebrangulo?) had already been released. She'd gotten well
without the help of a doctor, thanks to a promise made to
Saint Michael the Angel.

"It seems there's another epidemic of typhoid in Maceió."

That morning the nurse had told her that the man who
sold airplane tickets had killed himself with one shot, and it
was thought he'd done so because he'd spent the money,
which was supposed to be turned over to the owners of the
company, on a tramp. But it could also be a case of murder.
When the nurse had left, promising to get her a pack of
cigarettes, she'd lain down again, head high on the hard
pillow.

The death of Alexandre Viana didn't affect her. In the
first place, death was one thing which in no way interested
her. Partially cured of her venereal diseases, she passed hours
alone, thinking about the realization, which she supposed to
be near (and yet would never be consummated), of her big
dream: to be accepted at Dina's Place. This had been her
greatest desire since she'd arrived in Maceió, and the fact
that it had never been fulfilled seemed only to increase her
will to attain it. In the second place, she could never imagine
that she'd passed part of a night with the suicide. It had
been some weeks after her arrival in Maceió. She'd left the
house to get some ice cream but the man didn't have coconut, her favorite, and she'd given it up, had wandered about
the neighboring streets, going as far as the Cock Pit. Alexandre Viana, who'd just lit a cigarette and was expelling two
fine eddies of smoke from his nostrils, had approached her.

In the bedroom of the whorehouse, having already taken off
her outer garments, wearing only a slip, she had reached
for the vial of scent to perfume her armpits, thinking to be
acting like a lady of high society. He'd embraced her, raised
her slip and, stroking her buttocks, had made a certain
proposition. She'd limited herself to say, softly but with a
surprising firmness, in which there was perhaps a certain
professional ethic or even obstinacy: "Only the normal way,
nothing else." Her answer had satisfied him, he hadn't insisted, and they'd gone to bed. Upon leaving, he'd been
amused by her wine-colored bathrobe, had gone so far as
to say that she appeared a married woman, and this had
made her very proud.

She didn't know he was dead, and what's more, wouldn't
have recognized him if she'd been permitted to enter the
mortuary and look at Alexandre Viana's face. His eyes, of
a green-tinged brown, presented a moist luminosity; and a
part of the face, at the height of the right ear, had been
transformed into a repellent bloody mass, possessing little of
humanity. She never could have recognized him because already the tenuous recollection of his face, fine and cunning
as a fox's snout, had been forever erased from her memory.

Nor was she sure he was the one she had told her story to.
Was it the man encountered near the Cock Pit, the one who
had made her that proposition (or had that been another
one?) and whose left index fingernail was almost entirely
covered by a fine brown nicotine stain? Or was it the fat cus-
tomer she'd been with the following night? One of them had
asked her, after the screw, how she'd come to end up there.

She knew that many men asked these questions only to
rest while they gathered strength to do it again—and that
the story itself had elements which excited them, which
made the desire rise up again in those stretched out whore-
mongering bodies and attentive eyes. He (the man from the
Cock Pit or the fat character with the extraordinarily hairy

hands and pug nose) had offered her a cigarette, a Blue
Yolanda, and had even lit it, a courtesy which enchanted her
and provoked within her a certain meteoric desire to do it
again, for pure pleasure, as if she weren't in a whorehouse
and didn't pay for bed and board.

She'd told everything—not a linear story like those she
sometimes had a chance to read in the newspapers or in the
pamphlets sold at the Little Bird Market. These, though she
didn't know it, were stories by nineteenth-century novelists
and their meek present-day imitators. It wasn't a story beginning with her birth and ending there in that bed in the
room of a house on Hay Street, but a story which began
anywhere and ended anywhere, unraveled and fragmentary,
in which the after preceded the before, the night's passing
held days and suns already extinct, tomorrow came before
confused, badly lived days before yesterday. It was, after all,
a tale badly told, and all mixed up, like a gypsy's or a horse-
thief's. She knew nothing of stories and besides, she wasn't
sure her life was really a story worthy of being narrated, like
those the blindmen sang in the markets and the popular
poets celebrated in the pamphlets written in round letters
and sold at the Little Bird Market.

Anyway, she'd told the man, in her substantial language
made up almost exclusively of names and verbs, of her mis-
adventures: where she'd come from and how she'd lost her
cherry, how she'd gone downhill until she'd entered that
house on Hay Street, carrying a tiny suitcase containing a
wine-colored bathrobe.

She'd begun the story on the road lined with anjico and
coral trees. The days were long. She, her father, her mother,
and two more brothers, were making the slow and continual
journey of creatures accustomed to the woods, like snakes
and possums. Along the conquered leagues the mornings became evenings, and the owls came once more to found their
empire on the palisades of the night. She and her family

slept beside the roads, next to xique-xique cactus and sagua-ros, and without dens they were poorer than the animals. Dawn refreshed their bodies, burnt by the successive suns. And when the first signs of day appeared in the sky, they arose and turned again to struggle a few leagues. They wanted to arrive in Tinhorão as soon as possible. The road was parched, dry, crossed by chameleons, and doves passed in the shining cloudless sky, heading to the lands of water. But soon the word of the prophet would be fulfilled in truth and splendor, and the parched burned brushland would become an orchard. The land would be distributed among the poor. There'd always be water in the reservoirs and water-holes, and fish in the creeks swollen to perennial rivers. In search of this miracle, they'd slept out in the open many a night. The children, tired and with empty stomachs, whimpered. In the landscape of dry rivers and the soaring flights of birds of prey, they walked leagues to get a cup of water from a thatched hut where a donkey or a goat was a sign of wealth. And they walked in the days flattened and twisted by the sun. They met with gypsies leading stolen horses to sell in the markets, corpses carried in hammocks, dirge singers, cowboys dressed in leather. They stopped to sleep. Awakened by the dawn, they took again to the road washed by the early light of day, and already flown over by falcons which, once in a while, dived into the thin brush in search of snakes. The household things weighed on their backs and in their hands, the hollowness in their stomachs acknowledged hunger, but the presentiment of impending purification helped them to bear the journey's privations and to go easy on the scant ration of brown sugar, flour, and dried meat which was their daily bread. The number of pilgrims increased. In the tiny processions of men bearing bundles of clothes and rawhide bags, and women carrying spraddle-legged children on their haunches, there were devotees covered with medals, the blind and crippled, purulents covered

with abcesses, and even a leper who had come down from
the rice fields of the São Francisco river, seeking salvation.
She never forgot, in all that mass of men, the bearded pil-
grim; they said he'd been a man of many possessions, and
had abandoned his family and farm to announce the return
of King Sebastian.* He wasn't going to Tinhorão—he had
his own path, looking for a place of stones to gather the
faithful and fulfill his mission on earth. The night unfolded,
the evening star came out in all its glory, the glowworms appeared and disappeared in the tangled roots of the trees, the
crickets chirped, the jujubes and pepper trees faded in the
darkening distances. In her animal silence, she closed her
eyes, lying on the hard ground. When she slept by starlight,
she was pursued by vagrant dreams and the flights of birds
of ill omen. The corral where the goats shit tiny purple balls
and the hedge fence she'd squatted by, gripped with stomach
pains, still came to her memory. Other images followed in
her mind as she pinched the man's second cigarette between
her fingers: the shack, the corral, the sleeping mats, the
clothes reeking of sweat. During that crossing, when the days
were so alike that the scorched landscape appeared to always be the same, sprouting forth from itself, the animals
which attracted her most were the geckos and sand lizards.
Once, drawn by a rustling of dry brush, she'd tried to run
after a sand lizard, and her father had screamed at her, full
of rage. One day, the succession of coral trees, Jew's thorns,
and pebbles came to an end, and they arrived in the promised
land, which had been green and moist, or so it appeared to
her now, in her short and treacherous memory. Her father
turned a few old bills, amassed from the sale of the house
and fields and kept tied in a handkerchief, over to the

* A Portuguese king (1554–1578) who disappeared in Africa. According
to superstition, he will someday return, bringing with him the Golden
Age.

prophet. He kneeled before the holy man, who blessed him, looking at him with bleary eyes. Someone had seen the prophet work one morning, helped by five hoes held by invisible hands. Once he'd whistled and little birds had come to eat from his palm. Tinhorão was full of people. The men planted corn, beans, and manioc. The children, fearful that the saint would punish them, went far away to play. One rainy night, she was sleeping on her mat when her father awakened her. The saint was calling. She went out on the muddy path, afraid she might step on toads. Soaked, she entered the saint's house and soon guessed the reason for the call. Not because she'd been told of certain habits and preferences of the prophet and was herself at an age when curiosity mingled with dread accompanied her, but simply because the excitement with which he received her, dressed in a cotton shirt and without pants, clarified his intentions. She screamed, struck by a fine pain (a knife pain) when the saint mounted her on the mat, and his beard scratched, and his asthmatic respiration grew louder. Afterwards she didn't know if the saint had said anything or if it all had passed in silence and scattered gestures. She returned home running. It was no longer drizzling in the night of wasps and somnambulant birds. Her father was already sleeping and didn't even ask her, the following day, or any other day, what the saint had wanted. She received other calls—she went, and the knifelike pain was less, only an itching in all her parts that later dissolved in a mixture of desire and nausea. One afternoon she was removing her clothes beside the river in order to take a bath (and nearby a pitiguari sang, the bird that announces the arrival of people from far away). She saw, among the tree trunks, a boy eyeing the quick white mullets in the green tinged water. It was she who impetuously summoned him with moist hands, made him approach, pulled him down by a thicket of sedge, she who dragged him on.

But the man listening to her wanted her to get to the end

of the story, perhaps he wanted to have another go or intended to leave. And she added that a detachment of police had invaded the fields, a lieutenant had given the prophet a thrashing with a cattle whip; her father had drawn his knife, killed a soldier, and vanished in the brush. At first she'd wandered about the ends of the earth, now one place, now another. She'd lived for a while with a brakeman (he was a widower with cauliflower ears and a cold frog's hand which made her shiver when he touched her body), later she'd set up with an old gossip who had been a cattle drover, until she'd ended up in Demolition Alley, in Penedo. For a few seconds there hovered in the room, almost materialized, an atmosphere created by the magic of that word, a word capable of evoking so many things: a city, a church in whose belfry there hung hundreds of bats, the treasures interred by the Dutch, the ceramic lizards in the street market, the water singing under the keel of a boat, the tiny flutes, cymbals, and bass drums of spontaneous music, lively and merry, the green valleys, the spreading bottom lands filled with rice fields, the muddy São Francisco river running among sand bars, its waters home to surubins, snook, piranhas and grunts. For her, the word Penedo meant principally the dying light of a small kerosene lamp in the narrow room of the house she'd stayed in in Demolition Alley, and the framed lithograph of St. Sebastian pierced by arrows hanging on the wall. And it was there that the traveling salesman (who was crazy about fried shrimp and beer) had made her a present of the wine-colored bathrobe. The man didn't want to do it again—he only wanted to listen, for sure he was one of those talkative types who like to ask questions, stick their noses into other peoples' lives. He'd thrown the cigarette butt on the tile floor, approached the basin to wash. She'd also gotten up and put on her bathrobe. She suddenly felt complete and worthy, like a lady after completing inevitable domestic rites. Seeing her with the bathrobe, the man—who, already in undershirt and shorts and sitting on the edge of the bed, was putting on his shoes—had smiled and made the comment which had made her feel so proud. She'd told him, then, that it had been the present of a traveling salesman in Penedo.

She hadn't told him that the great dream of her life was to use that bathrobe at Dina's, when she was finally accepted there. Nor did she confide to him that she'd already tried to get admitted there several times. She had called on the madam and explained her aspirations. Dina had eyed her from head to toe, as if evaluating an animal in the market, and all the while she had kept the tight-lipped expression of one who, in this inspection, didn't find any reason to accept the proposal. It wasn't possible, all the rooms were occupied. Even women from Recife had written her sending photographs, hoping for vacancies. Returning from those unsuccessful visits, she had chewed over her disappointment and couldn't find an explanation for her difficulties. As a whore, she was neither better nor worse than the others. She wasn't suffering then from any venereal disease—she'd picked up a case of crabs the week before, but had managed to get rid of them by shaving her pubic hairs and using a yellow salve the man at the drugstore had sold her. She considered herself clean and neat; she took a bath twice a day; she'd already received propositions to be somebody's mistress. Why didn't Dina want her at her place?

There, in the hospital bed, she asked the question again and soon calmed herself. She wasn't sure Dina didn't want her, and she was certain that one day she'd be accepted there. Before going to her room she'd have a glass of beer and dance with the man who had found her agreeable.

Within a few weeks she'd be free of the red permanganate douches and the injections, and she'd leave the hospital. She'd begin everything again; from somewhere she'd approach Dina's establishment, concentrically, with the patience of a bird of prey making ready for the kill. One day, dressed in the wine-colored bathrobe like somebody important, she would open the window of her room at Dina's and gaze languorously out upon that clear future morning from within her victory. It would be a luminous morning, and its emblems would be streetcars and wagons, sea and ships. She'd follow the steps of the passersby and hear the insistent matinal noises with the firm sensation that she'd triumphed in life.

In the next bed, the woman with black spots on her face and arms—a real clap-trap—was going on with the same old story, or perhaps another story, which emerged from within the first like an empty box stored inside another. Anyway, it was a story without beginning and without end; these were mere conventions demanded by the supposed rationality of a narrative which, like life itself, was irremediably condemned to be fragmentary, like a shattered mirror on the floor. She pretended to listen, even caught in the air a few threads of phrases, but her thoughts wandered far away, became lost on the parched paths of places disfigured by an unfaithful memory, a memory comparable to a succession of black spots in an empty landscape. She was lost in the thicket of an enigmatic, yet clearly seen future, where she situated herself, silent and merciful. She wouldn't need to change clothes, particularly since she felt herself already dressed for that full and shining day to come, wearing the wine-colored bathrobe the traveling salesman had given her in Penedo.

Once again she remembered his peal of laughter. Perhaps it was the man she'd met leaving the Cock Pit or the fat hairy man who had offered her a cigarette after the fuck, perhaps neither of them and, yes, a third who used a rubber or a fourth or a fifth. And she remembered the dwarf who used to visit her once a week, and who explored her body as slowly and industriously as an ant explores all the vastness of the earth or a beetle hovers tirelessly over the pistil of a flower or a pump sucks water from a well. With her eyes shut, she felt the dwarf upon her, loving her with his minute and frenetic dwarf's love; and as his ears grazed her breasts they became suddenly tumescent, as if in the sensuality of the moment there had stirred some unconfessable maternal instinct. How the dwarf was austere! From the tiny suspenders and two-toned shoes, from the linen clothing and the monogrammed shirt, from the red tie and the glasses, there emanated an unmistakable aura of severity, which went with his position as a businessman respected in the entire city. He was a numbers banker, owner of almost a whole street down by the Harbor Warehouse, possessor of immense bank deposits and friend of the Interventor and the Chief of Police. Still with her eyes closed, and not wanting to open them, so as not to provoke the rupture of the hallucination which kept her floating in space in a kind of spongy splendor, she admitted that with the dwarf she'd come more than with other men, even when she gave herself to them disposed to feel, and not repeating a succession of mechanical gestures and movements. Really, it was useless to deny it, she'd come more with the dwarf, in prolonged and gelatinous spasms which made her moan, changed into water and fury. Feeling him explore her like an ant or a beetle, and touched by his thick dog's tongue, she admitted that in truth, she'd only come with him. When she closed her eyes, the dwarf became a giant, transformed into a trunked animal. Minutes later, enveloped in the bathrobe, she'd tried to hide from herself the truth that had blazed in her spasm and forced her to recognize a touch of vileness and bestiality in her life (as if to come with a dwarf were a sin, an unconfessable abnormality).

But that laughing man with the cigarette hadn't had the force and the intimate tenacity to be preserved untouched in her memory, perhaps no man in the world was endowed with that virtue, only someone in a dream like a shoe in a shoe-box. Seeing her with the bathrobe, he'd laughed, had recognized in her the proprietary and domestic air of married women who rode in cars and lived in houses where there were flower gardens and caged birds and chairs with cushions and a record circling inflexibly on the victrola. For a second, no more, she'd closed her eyes and felt as if she were already at Dina's, fully invested with her compact and future dignity, making measured and languorous gestures, slowly raising an arm without the sleeve of the bathrobe slipping down to her elbow, accepting a cold glass of beer offered by a lawyer or a judge.

"It was really suicide. A police investigator told me so there in the store."

The nurse had returned, with a pack of cigarettes.

"The city's full of American sailors."

═ THE MAN BEHIND THE COUNTER ═

n the streetcar, two lawyers were discussing the fox's death.

"It was an act of savagery."

"I disagree with my distinguished colleague. To me, it was the natural reaction of a handful of people representing civilization." Privately, he reproached his hirsute companion, who was using a nauseating brilliantine.

Sparks flew from a locomotive whistling by the station platform.

"But to kill a poor defenseless animal? They could have captured it and offered it to a zoo. Or perhaps returned it to the woods."

By the gate of the Bishop's Palace, a pious-faced zealot, her breast covered with scapulars, was waving to a priest on the other side of the street. A wagon's wheels squeaked on the paving stones washed by the hot sun.

"In the first place, we don't have a zoo . . ."

"In Recife they do. They could have sent it there. And I'll bet they don't have a fox. Brazilians think animals from other countries are important, lions, elephants, and tigers.

And they think our monkeys aren't as good as the African ones. An inferiority complex."

From his pocket he took a cigarette case displaying his initials. A married woman in Recife had given it to him on his graduation—an old affair he liked to recount in bars and notary offices, adding a few purely imaginary erotic details.

"But foxes really do like to eat chickens. I remember once, when I was a kid, the chicken coop there at home was a real cemetery one morning, feathers everywhere . . ."

"I still maintain that it was cruel."

When the streetcar turned the corner, the almost white sand dunes appeared, advancing toward the blue sea. In the houses worn down by time the furtive shadow of life flowed—faces, gestures, voices which rose, lowered, mixed together, melted into an incoherent babble, weaving an arbitrary carpet of forms, colors, and sounds in the clear air. Nevertheless, there was something inaccessible stamped in the faces and attitudes of the people leaning out of the windows or strolling in the streets. That which was most apparent and exterior in them wasn't sufficient for their identification. It could be said that each carried a secret, gave himself over to a secret labor like a spider which, feigning indolence, casts into the empty air a capricious and invisible web, pertinaciously investing in it all his expectations.

We're all spiders, or centipedes hiding under beds—under the secret of beds which only at night are opened to the profound truth of beings which love and dream, and dash themselves against the walls of other bodies and seek to enshroud their loneliness in the indifferent sheets—or among the rotten timbers of cellars and attics, thought the lawyer, remembering the stories of his love affair so often related to his cronies at the courthouse. And how we lie! he mentally added, eyeing the statue of the Viscount of Sinimbu and a few children (one on a bicycle) who were running among the pottery trees. His former mistress from Pernambuco had been married to a barber, a submissive cuckold besides, and not to a sergeant in the military police, whom he portrayed as jealous and bellicose. Nor was it true that the trysts occured in her house, on the nights the imaginary husband was on duty. They took place in rented rooms, not only because she had four small children, but also because she feared the neighborhood gossip.

"I respect my colleague's opinion, but . . ."

Sitting on the bench behind, the man who wrote anonymous letters listened to the conversation of the two lawyers with his ears pricked. His gaze strayed to a lighter beached on the shore.

"What about Alexandre Viana's suicide?"

His nostrils dilated as he sniffed the corrosive sea air—the odor which, connecting Maceió to the entire universe, impregnated even the records of the notary offices.

"It's going around that it was the Brotherhood." There was a thrill of terror in his voice. It was as if he feared that his spider or centipede's name was also included on the secret list of that invisible tribunal. After all, he didn't know if he was innocent or guilty. Even if he were innocent, would he be safe?

"No, that's all been cleared up. He killed himself with one shot from a revolver. Such a young man, with a good job—and a future. Doing such a crackpot thing. And he left a young son."

On the sidewalk, a boy was going by with a bird in a cage. It was a rice finch.

"He had a mistress."

The streetcar reached the beach. The man on the back bench tried to concentrate his attention on the letter he was mentally composing. Your Reverence? Excellency? Reverend Bishop? He'd decided to denounce a certain canon who, according to information which had reached his ears, was sleeping with his maid. But he was stuck on that detail—how to address the Bishop? There was no one he could ask.

"Is my distinguished colleague aware that man is the only animal which commits suicide?" He examined his shoes. Gonguila had shined them that morning. How they gleamed! On the beach, a boy was flying a kite.

"What a sun, hey?"

The day was full, sea green. The waves ran, one after another, and the whiteness of their foam came to dissolve itself on the beach.

"That's an American ship out there."

"I've seen some sailors wandering about. But what a view!"

With mincing steps, a vulture came near the water's edge.

"It's a wonderful view. There's nothing like it in the Northeast. And well-travelled people, who have been out of the country, guarantee that we have the most beautiful beaches in the world. Look at that blue sky."

A ship wheezed. The sea was like a great open door, painted entirely blue. He, however, belonged to the race of those who stay, of those animals which remain captives even with the cage door open. He was certain he would never leave.

"I don't doubt it, but about the suicide . . ."

A vulture flew low over a black roof, almost touching it.

"Look at Professor Serafim Gonçalves' house. Look at the library. They say he leaves the windows open to impress whoever passes by."

Soft and tepid waves rolled loosely in from the calm sea.

"Everyone has his vanity. But he's a great lawyer. And he's going to have a brilliant political career. He'll wind up being senator or governor of this state."

At the stop, the motorman waited for a blindman, aided by his anemic little guide, to get down. An old woman got off too, carrying a basket of sapodilla.

"But as I was saying, irrational animals don't commit suicide. Only man, who is rational, kills himself. Don't you think there's a link between suicide and the use of reason?"

The other recalled a conversation between chief judges, overheard the evening before when he'd gone to the courthouse to begin an appeal.

"Free will . . ."

His companion removed his fogged glasses, cleaned them with his handkerchief, nodded his head.

"Just what I was getting at. In effect, free will gives man the liberty to choose his own death."

The streetcar had turned up a twisting street. The man who wrote anonymous letters looked at the tiled fronts of the old two-storied houses. In one of them, Dina's Place was functioning. He imagined naked women smelling of lotion, orgies which came to an end only with the sunrise. That was how he pictured it when he jacked off in his room at the Old Palace.

"This is the essential problem: man's liberty and its limits. Don't you think . . . ?"

The streetcar had halted at the stop by the Chamber of Commerce. The man on the back bench jumped down. The warehouse was across the street, with its sacks, barrels, and strings of onions. A portrait of Getúlio Vargas hung on the yellowed wall. He could hear the ships' whistles from behind the counter. It was as if his universe ended there, in the splashing of the dark thick water beneath the warehouse pilings, in the crabs' dens, in the stench of the sea air entering his nostrils, in the bills of lading which passed through his hands, in the iron gratings being eaten away by rust, in the sacks of sugar waiting to be loaded, in the molasses stained floor. Your Excellency? Reverend? Eminence? No, Eminence was only for Cardinals. Immobile on the curb, he waited for a truck to pass, and looked at one of the two-storied houses. A green-eyed mulatto, leaning over her balcony railing, was observing the movement in the street. That

night, if he felt the urge to beat off, he'd have to remember
her—remember her hair, disheveled as of someone just
awakened, the cotton bathrobe and shaved armpits. He'd
close his eyes and see her with her legs spread wide. Bishop.
He crossed the street, toward the waiting counter. But he
didn't write the anonymous letters at work.

It wasn't at the warehouse counter, by the sticky sacks of
sugar, that he wrote the letters. There he limited himself to
observing, hearing, listening to conversations, and contem-
plating the black-hulled, white-decked ships, while his mind
unrolled, as if it were a ball of yarn, the phrase he would
write at night, seated at the little table of his bachelor bedroom in the Old Palace. He was going to have to move from
there, sooner or later, as it was to be demolished so a modern
building could be constructed in its place. And the phrase
came and went, it stretched, became feral and succinct, something strictly informational: *My distinguished fellow citizen's wife is cheating on him. A friend.* As for the expression
"distinguished fellow citizen," he'd read it in a birthday note
which had come out in the *Alagoas Gazette,* had liked it, and
had decided to use it in his next anonymous letter, which
looked as though it would be directed to a dentist. Picking
his teeth with a match he'd sharpened with his fingernail, he
thought about his secret function, revealing secrets, denounc-
ing everything done on the sly in the city.

From the depths of his childhood came the memory of the
night when he'd observed the stratagem of concealment for
the first time. He was lying in his bed in the room without
a light when he heard someone knock softly on the street
door. He was frightened. Who could it be? He wanted to call
his mother to come and protect him from that faint, early-
morning knocking. But suddenly he heard the sound of slip-
pers in the next bedroom, and steps moving away in the direction of the living room. A gust of wind entered the house,
dissolved in the livid walls and lath and plaster. Then he

heard the door being closed, cautious footsteps, his mother's
voice again. He closed his eyes because his mother's steps were
directed toward his room. He sensed the door being opened
and the familiar smelling body standing next to him, a hand
pulling the cretonne sheet closer to his face. The tremulous
light from the night lamp his mother had brought gave him
the urge to open his eyes, to show he wasn't sleeping. As
soon as she left, he again raised his lids and listened to the
tiniest rustlings. It could be said that the house was full of
movement, though it was nothing more than a sequence of
snaps and small prudent sounds. His mother's footsteps went
to the kitchen, he heard a stream of water falling into a
basin. She returned, and slowly closed the door to the adja-
cent room. He accompanied the incomprehensible sounds,
each of which had to have a secret meaning. There were
shoes being dropped, whispers, the mattress giving way beneath an unfamiliar weight. What could they be doing? In
a little while he heard something like a struggle, the thread
of disordered breathing; it was as if the rain were beating
on the roof tiles. Afterwards there was a lengthy silence, and
he fell asleep. The following day he still asked himself what
mystery that could be. He'd almost related the strange happening to a kid from the neighborhood, but he remembered
his mother coming to verify that he was sleeping, and that
she had said nothing about the nocturnal visit at breakfast.
A few days later, she bought some khaki cloth and made
him a new suit. Because of the happiness he felt in his new
clothes, he seldom recalled the episode.

Once, he'd wanted to play with some children who had
come to live near his house, and one of them had repulsed
him: "I won't play with a whore's son." For many days he'd
wanted to ask his mother the meaning of the words which
kept him from making certain acquaintances. He had no
father. On one occasion he'd asked about him, and his
mother had responded that he'd died. He decided that a

whore's son was any child whose father had died. But it didn't take him long to discover his mistake. A boy, conversing with him on the corner sidewalk, said he was going to study for free because he was the son of a widow. His father had died of tuberculosis. There was naturally a big difference between a whore's son and a widow's son. Widows' husbands died of tuberculosis.

Later, there came the years at St. Dominick's Orphanage. He'd become a young man, finished the accounting course, arranged a job, and his eyes turned to fill themselves with ships, and the whistles that announced sailings and voyages died in his ears. He hadn't married and he lived in that rented room, in the Old Palace, where he'd wound up after a few years in the neighborhood of the Sheep's Armpit.

Stretched out in bed, he listened to the wind on the tin roof. He wasn't sleepy. He rolled over, lay on his stomach, scratched himself. Was it the sound of the tin roof or of a basin being filled with water at that obscure point in his childhood which could never be erased? Worm-eaten doors slammed. Rats walked through puddles of piss. The wind flayed the banana trees. A bird spider melted into the shadow like a lethal jewel. *Illustrious fellow citizen: Your wife is . . .* He'd learned where to place the pronouns and the accent marks while at St. Dominick's Orphanage. Thus, he could take pride in his letters. He made no gross errors though he admitted that his spelling wasn't always correct. He'd never become familiar with the new orthographic reform.

He always left at sunset, before the warehouse closed. He would take the streetcar, get off at the Official Clock, and mix with the groups of acquaintances which were busy shredding reputations. He listened more than he spoke. While he was listening to the unending conversations which shots fired by a Brotherhood gunman might suddenly disperse, his eyes accompanied the women who crossed the street and vanished into the shoe shops and dry goods stores.

They followed the steps of the men who entered the Commercial Billiards and, between the tables, went to the rear, disappearing into the area reserved for playing poker. *Noble friend. The manager of your firm is addicted to poker. Just yesterday he lost . . .* He craned his neck to see better and lowered his head so his ears could capture a word murmured in a low voice.

After various years of acquaintance with all the groups spread out along Main Street, he knew which were the most observant, which ones dealt with and unraveled affairs, the ones able to divulge the information he lacked (since he passed almost the entire day at the warehouse counter and couldn't follow the adulterers and grafters around). While all about him they dealt with the delivery and shipment of merchandise, and bills of lading and dispatches circulated, he cunningly formed the phrase: *Distinguished fellow citizen: Your husband arranged a house for a tramp on Sand Street.* In his room there was always a good supply of blue commercial envelopes and large sheets of paper (each sheet was cut to make four letters), as well as stamps. That way he didn't need to show the clerks at the post office window the envelope, where the name of the recipient was printed in letters like newsprint. He would put it directly in the box and return to the warehouse. Before entering, he'd pause in the doorway. He was like a spider, condemned to the eternal torment of expectation. His gaze wandered from the high wall of the customs shed to a flight of seagulls hovering not only over houses, warehouses, black pilings which never rotted, Dina's Place, the Excise Office and fish traps, but also over the granular and odorous substance of the moment, which enveloped the naval displays in the next square, the white columns and steps of the Chamber of Commerce building, the aggressive street stones still unpolished by time, men's feet, and the wheels of vehicles, and the clear air where the scent of salt brine mixed with that of piles of sacked sugar at the rear of the depositories. The crooked street, with the underseas telegraph agency, the brothels located in ancient two-storied houses, the insurance companies, the consular agencies, the banks, the warehouses, the houses of company representatives, the greasy bars, everything seemed to be nourished by all that came from the sea: people, ships, paper, wine, algae.

At the beginning of the seventeenth century the only signs of settlement in that region were the slave quarters of a sugar plantation called Massavó, next to which a chapel had been raised under the invocation of St. Gonçalo. Ships which were then the height of modernity (and today could only be found in albums or history books) paused before the split-level cannibalistic panorama. The lower level was an expanse of marshy swampland and the upper level was formed by the end of a tableland which penetrated deeply into the interior. Pirates used to descend from their schooners and hookers to look for brazilwood. Whaling ships stalked the apparently empty sea. When Manuel Antônio Duro received a grant of eight hundred braças* of land from Gabriel Soares, high mayor of Santa Maria Madalena da Lagoa do Sul (which would become the city of Alagoas, first capital of the province), he constructed in Pajuçara, facing the sea and the light of day, a brick house mentioned in a public document dated the 25th of November in the year of Our Lord 1611. This house constituted the first sign of the settlement of Maceió, a city which still didn't exist during the Dutch dominion in Brazil, or was of such little importance that none of the detailed Dutch maps of the period registered it. Certainly this sugar plantation had grown due to its proximity to the ocean. By the bay, it slowly became a port. Clandestine in the beginning, it attracted French corsairs and permitted the embarkation of sugar without the fury of

* The braça is equivalent to 3,562 square meters.

the tax collectors augmenting the price. This stimulated the commerce of the Azorians, possibly the first settlers of the floodlands and tableland, who in the beginning had been interested in mining and looking for gold.

The tongue of water looked upon by the individual called Antônio Duro wasn't yet the ostensibly commercial sea of the beginning of the nineteenth century. Then the harbor gave birth to a regular trade, and the first shops and wine cellars, with their counters and shelves and the haggling of peddlars and wholesalers appeared there where he (thinking about another anonymous letter) found himself. Clothes, sweetmeats, cotton, timbers for the building of houses and the construction of ships, leathers, tobacco, corn, rice and beans were brought from the interior by pack trains and ox carts led by slaves, and from there in Jaraguá—whose commerce bought them either directly or merely on consignment—they passed to the bellies of the sailing ships which carried them to Pernambuco and Bahia. Of all these exportable products, that which came in greatest quantity, the most tangible in a land open to so many other seeds and shoots, was sugar. Because of this, even today, Jaraguá reeks of sugar. It smells as much of the sugar loaded in the Lloyd and Costeira freighters and in the foreign ships, which for a few days infuses the stevedores with a sumptuous vision of the fullness of the Earth, as of that ancient and immemorial sugar which had attracted the attention of the royal tax collector. The city of Alagoas, the county seat, followed with jealousy and fear the development of the village by the sea which, thanks to its harbor, was contributing to the decay and decadence of the old French Port. The county seat's fear was justified: on the 5th of December, 1815, Prince Dom João, regent of the kingdom of Portugal, in the name of his mother, Dona Maria the Mad, signed the charter creating the town of Maceió, dismembering it from the Villa of Alagoas. The three councilmen and the procurator elected when

Maceió achieved its emancipation and commenced to organize itself, the mayor who watched over the order of the new town, the two ordinary judges, the juvenile court judge, and the two notaries of the judicial public and records, these men who were the most important authorities of the population of five thousand souls, all felt the scent of sugar which impregnated the air and which was transformed into piles of coins guarded in leather chests whose gold colored bindings meant ostentation and wealth. And thus, in this atmosphere marked by the anxiety for progress, there had arisen the courthouse, jail, and brick pillory which, in the chapel patio, symbolized the town, raising its sign of law, order, and justice against bestiality, rapacity, and crime. These and other institutions were constructed at the cost of the inhabitants in accordance with the charter which the fat Dom João, after a well garnished luncheon of cockerels, had signed in the name of his mother, Dona Maria the Mad, on that 5th of December of 1815.

On the 9th of December in 1839, the city of Maceió had become the provincial capital thanks to its maritime and topographical position, becoming the seat of government, of the Assembly, the Provincial Treasury, and higher education. Now, more than a century later, this scent of sugar still remained, as much in the ancient Pillory Square where the city was born from a sugar plantation as in lanes and alleys losing themselves in the direction of Mundaú Lagoon.

This smell of past and present, this age-old and sticky smell of sugar, had permeated street stones, portraits of highborn ancestors descended from highwaymen and prostitutes banished by the king of Portugal, streetcar runningboards, the expediters' breaths, ornamental moldings of two-story houses, church tiles, the dirty walls of houses sheltering spiders and centipedes, trunks full of lace, requisitions circulating in government offices, pianos, clothes, the saints in their shrines. It penetrated dreams, furniture varnish, charters, cigar boxes

containing candy and coins, even the people's souls. The
girls' bodies, when they were nude, also had this scent of
sugar which, despite its milled and immemorial impregna-
tion, didn't always manage to sweeten the hardness and
cruelty of their spirits, nor turn less violent the native and
explosive irascibility of those appetites and whims which led
to bloodshed—perhaps sugared blood, laden with that uninterrupted honey of time which attracted flies. Certainly,
even the statue of the Viscount of Sinimbu (the great statesman of the empire, cause for pride in every Alagoan though
only a few of them might know for sure what he'd done and
why he'd been covered with glory and such monumental and
tarnished oblivion) in the square bearing his name, had
something sugared in its patina. The same substance was
found in the jawbreakers sold from trays on the corners and
in sweetmeats kept in compote jars in houses where the
buzzing of flies increased surprisingly after meals. Flies
which, in a city without sewers, and built on the excrement
of its inhabitants, were carriers of typhoid or carriers of
nothing.

*Eminent fellow citizen: Abusing your trust, your part-
ner* . . . Within the vast and shining magnificence of the
afternoon, the seagulls continued flying over the world of
the port, ships' flags, life, barges and lighters at rest on the
beach, the dull splashing of the water beneath warehouses
on pilings, two-story houses where brothels operated. A
clarity at once yellow and blue enveloped the geographical
coordinates: 9°40′18″ south latitude and 35°44′00″ west of
Greenwich, to the scant altitude of five meters above the
hypnotic sea and its absurd, watery logic. The afternoon, sustained by the beauty of universal harmony, dressed with a
vibrant and tepid light the statues of Marshal Deodoro da
Fonseca, proclaimer of the Republic, and Marshal Floriano
Peixoto, its consolidator. Both statues transmitted a majestic
sensation to the children of the school groups, the sensation

that Alagoas, birthplace of these two subjects fit for Plutarch, and home of a world famous coconut tree known as the ostrich's Adam's apple, was the center of the universe. This despite its being the second smallest state in Brazil, next to Sergipe, and fifty-two times smaller than Amazonas. "Good things come in small packages," said the teachers, calling the attention of the sleepy-eyed children with fingers in their mouths to the glory of Alagoas. On certain occasions they were obliged to sing the state anthem: "O Alagoas, radiant orb in the morning sky/Gracious star 'mongst sister stars/ Always first in the Republic's eye." The children didn't know the meaning of "radiant orb," and many of them, correcting the words and the teacher, sang "Republic's sty," caught up in a sudden and unquenchable civic enthusiasm which would surely be soothed with age.

A fly buzzed. Or was it a bee? *Illustrious friend. The cashier of your prestigious establishment gave his wife, on that virtuous woman's birthday, a jewel worth* . . . The seagulls carried on, soaring above the great full afternoon made of earth and water and clouds displacing themselves in the direction of the sun. And the evening closed in, pink and blue. The depots closed their doors, making the agitation of the waves seem greater in the silence. The crabs took refuge in their black dens. The wind rustled in the ships, rotting since the past century, sunken in the mud of the lagoons. The termite queens came to rest on the sticky islands. The coconut groves danced. The streets were becoming deserted, though one could hear the clatter of a few billiard balls rolling on green felt, the sound of a samba at Dina's, and the shriek of a window being cracked open by a nun at the hospital. The chatter of those who traded loose talk around the Official Clock and in the bars diminished. Then came the night and then the dawn and the vultures took flight and hunted carrion. The branches of the pottery trees shivered, touched by the sea breeze. Immobile in the shadows, the centipedes anticipated the morning's advance across the floor of the universe.

The man from behind the counter came down the steps of the Old Palace after having his morning coffee. (He'd freed a fly buzzing inside a sugar shaker.) While he walked, he noted the increasing number of beggars appearing on the sidewalks, as if the sun had called to free them of fleas and mange or cure them of ulcers and elephantiasis. On a wall, someone had sketched a swastika, an old drawing in pitch, which the rains could not erase.

Passing by the police headquarters, heading to the streetcar stop (during the ride he would listen to the two lawyers' conversation), he heard the roar of motorcycles. He already knew, by then, the news of the day. During his coffee, Guabiraba had told him of Alexandre Viana's death.

THE CEMETERY

The cemetery was by the sea. A white wall separated it from the line of coconut palms. The soft sand, trampled by the feet of those attending Alexandre Viana's burial, was the ancient dune sand tamed so the dead could be interred in a territory where earth and water met. An American sailor—strong, tall, blond—was taking pictures of the headstones.

In the open grave, a crab appeared and then disappeared, as if frightened by the spectacle of the men who'd come to bury the suicide. The Latin phrase from over the cemetery gate hovered in Professor Serafim Gonçlaves' mind. It advised the Alagoans that they were dust, and that to dust they would return. But evidently, few Alagoans knew Latin well enough to translate and absorb it with their spirits, which ravenously loved both life and money.

Turning to gaze upon the grave, Professor Serafim Gonçalves saw something whitish and viscous which, with its rings, moved like a tiny accordion. It must have been a worm. Though the afternoon sun was strong, and reddish spatters were beginning to streak the blue and white sky, many of those present had come dressed in dark clothing—as if death deserved respect and called for austere colors. The clarity, coming from the sky and sucked up by the sea foam, accentuated the brilliance of the gold foil surrounding the coffin's violet cross.

Opening the way with his protruding stomach squeezed into a double-breasted suit coat of tropical beige, Armando Wucherer, poet, the celebrated author of "Songs of Tedium," approached Professor Serafim Gonçalves. They were silent for a moment, eyeing the casket which was slowly being lowered into the grave by ropes. But soon the poet wanted to relieve the solemnity of the moment, which let itself be strewn with everything and nothing, like the births and deaths of men. With his hoarse voice and a malicious gleam in his blue eyes:

"A judge was dismissed in Paraíba because he had a mistress. We should call him to come and live in Maceió. Here, almost the entire bar has someone on the side!" And he smiled, the restrained smile of someone who is at a funeral and desires only to disguise the impiety of life.

Other voices disintegrated in the silence cadenced by the sound of the gravediggers. The presence of death stimulated dialogues. One, in another's face: "But, isn't there a priest at this funeral?"

And the wind. And the sand. And the whiteness of the luminous day slowly eating away at life. And those dunes which had been the first sign of land when Admiral Pedro Álvares Cabral, sailing the curved sea, had discovered Brazil, beginning in the cry of a sailor high on a mast, in a distant green stain, in seagulls flying alone as in the beginning of the world.

"Suicides have no right to the sacraments, didn't you know?"

A long, long way off, a shred of cloud frayed away. The screech of a streetcar on the tracks. The coconut palms sang.

Buzzards with full craws nodded on the rooftops.

"You mean to say that . . ."

Guabiraba pricked his ears, bummed a cigarette.

"Was it really suicide? It's going around about the Brotherhood."

The lawyer stiffened. A reddish haired type, rough look-ing, seemed to be measuring him with his eyes.

I'm not innocent, he reflected. It was—it wasn't, I live telling stories in every office around. I lie like crazy. I'm guilty and I carry everybody's guilt with me. If the Brother-hood assassinates me, I'll be paying for me and for the others. He looked at the other mourners: faces without innocence, greedy eyes, mouths that astutely held silence and lies, avid hands which since childhood had learned to clutch money, and their ties squeezed throats which someday would be slit.

"Camões, running into Bocage one day . . ."

That redhaired character is a hired gunman, Hortêncio's bodyguard. Am I looking at my future murderer? The law-yer's attention was diverted by the blond sailor, who was snapping pictures of the graves.

Now the sea was only a far away murmur, as if it were retreating from the dunes and the coagulated algae. The tumult of the hesitant waves dissipated in silence and clarity. Interred in the salty sand, the dead must have felt even more the presence of death, deprived of the immemorial rustle of life and movement which, among the warehouses and the shipdecks, the houses and the blue sky, unrolled like an un-ending ball of yarn.

"The Mayor of Santana do Ipanema told me this morning that a new saint has appeared there in the back country and is knocking up every virgin in sight. The man's obsession is popping cherries and saying he's going to distribute the plantation owners' land."

A lizard scurried between the tombstones.

"The best cure for gonorrhea is cornsilk tea, you can drink it."

A few hands lowered, seized fistfuls of that yellow sand, millennially moistened by ocean waters, and threw them on the coffin.

For an instant, the nearby ocean waves roared in a festive affirmation of life and movement, color and light, in a muted canticle that unfolded, filling the expanse of the mourners' dread there at Alexandre Viana's funeral. The earth tossed on the casket, covering the purple cross and gold foil, reminded the bystanders that they were dust beneath the shrieking wind—and that to dust they would return. In the soft earth, neighbor to waters and the strident sea, their bodies would be visited by crabs and crayfish, as if they had drowned.

"Yesterday I screwed a broad I picked up in the Cock Pit. What a cunt! She was shaggy as a bird spider." Something ancestral and cannibalistic vibrated in the phrase, as if there reechoed in it the savage customs of the forest Indians who, mindful of their cannibal ethics, had transformed Bishop Sardinha into Sunday dinner and, because of this, had been massacred by the colonists.

"What you really ought to screw is a green-eyed mulatto girl who comes from Porto Real do Colégio."

They wanted to clutch at life, to seize the threads of existence which were fraying in memories bruised by the spectacle of that interment. They paced their tiny mental cages, while the sea roared nearby—blue and white, blue and white—and eternally victorious like death. Startled, they let themselves be overcome by the thought that life was an accident, unimportant, uncertain, and transitory, comparable to a fluttering fly trying to approach the nostrils of a corpse or the scattered hairs on a hand holding the strap of a funeral bier.

In Maceió, in the drugstores where they sold potassium

permanganate and rubbers, or in the black books of the registry offices, books that consecrated the allotment of man's misery and ambition, whether in land or hard cash; in the fat and twisted angels of the churches and in the confessionals where the old and unending stories of youthful masturbation, covetousness, and adultery unfolded, in love and litigation, in truth and falsehood, everything seemed to occur by chance. Perhaps in Alexandre Viana's suicide there pulsed the intention of converting the accidental into something respectable and illustrious like a law, or a charter similar to that of the Brotherhood, the great secret tribunal of Alagoas. Whatever, he had cleared the obstacle, leapt the great empty space like a horse, to transform himself, on that voyage without return, into dust violated by the hunger of the crabs. Or perhaps he had become, for all time, and even beyond all didactic or measurable time, pure essence kept in unexpected vacuums, preserved in a limbo of ice or fire, and perpetuating, in the eternity of the always renewed and germinating suns and galaxies, the sign of his senseless gesture. In that gesture he'd tried to reconcile all the extremes, servitude and liberty, the reeking cage which had appeared in his childhood and the fire between Enaura's legs.

A tall lanky individual was praising the suicide:

"He was a smart boy. He could have left Maceió, had himself a career out there."

Beyond the dunes, the ships' gangplanks lay on the immense sea. But who would leave?

"Maceió is one big cemetery. In truth, all of us are already dead and buried."

In their hearts, they felt themselves glued to the streets, the lighthouse, the sound of the sea, the squeaking stairways leading to the whorehouses. And they loved the heat of that land like snakes love their nests of stone.

But Alexandre Viana had faded; and his nonexistence wandered in the hallways of nothingness.

"And he was a hard worker. At seven o'clock, he was already on the job, at the agency counter."

His name had been set loose from his body and frozen soul; and it also sought the path of the wind and dust, beyond the dunes and the ships' gangplanks.

"They're talking about embezzlement . . ." It was the voice of a pharmaceutical products salesman who spent his days visiting doctors' offices. In his aquamarine worsted suit (with shiny trouser bottoms) he was feeling the heat. He wondered who would take Alexandre Viana's place.

He'd managed to cross the river; on the banks of the other shore there were no trinkets, no rusty or twisted crosses. The ample deception of his life had come undone. His spoils were dust. His inventory was the wind.

"I don't believe it. He killed himself because of that tramp." Guabiraba raised his blinking fool's eyes to the speaker.

The conversation wandered in circles, like a merry-go-round pony. The sound of the bruised earth filling the grave diminished. Some of the funeral company idled among the crooked crosses, trampled ugly flowers, read names, looked at faded pictures, diverted themselves in a sinister stroll, as if the old deaths, already evaporated, erased the stain Alexandre Viana's burial had left on the sand.

Esteemed fellow citizen: Your most excellent consort . . . He was there too, to overhear the dialogue which cast doubt on the suicide's honesty. To be truthful, he hadn't known him personally—he'd only been accustomed to seeing him behind the airline agency counter. He remembered (and perhaps it was a memory created by death) that once, in Zanotti's Bar, they'd both stood side by side, waiting for the ice to be crushed for their drinks. Certainly there'd been other occasions when their paths had crossed: in the Gate of the Sun, in the Helvética, on a streetcar. But from the stirred-up memory there surfaced no episode when they'd exchanged

words. However, he'd pretended to be a friend of Alexandre
Viana's in order to get off work earlier. And there he was.

His mother was buried in that cemetery. Her tomb was
one of the last, close to the wall by the beach. However, he
didn't feel disposed to go and look at it. He didn't even visit
it on All Souls' Day. With his mother's death, he'd experienced a mixed feeling of tranquility and relief. He'd considered himself finally alone and free, able to exercise his
secret vocation as an observer, keeping his ears open to truth
and calumny, capturing the signs of distant movements and
concocting, in the Old Palace, the letters which disturbed or
disordered existences, producing revulsion and bitterness,
becoming the emblems of degradation. Visiting his mother's
grave was the same as returning to a time already extinct,
listening again in the thick night to the same ambiguous
whispers which had disturbed his childhood, to face once
more a creature who had escaped his thirst for judgment. She
had never spoken his father's name. She'd limited herself to
saying that he'd died.

Still, on those afternoons when the ships whistled in the
port of Jaraguá, and a few unknown faces appeared in
the depots near the Customs house, he was assaulted by the
almost certainty that his father had been a traveler. He had
been one of those creatures of passage who never warm any
seat for long and leave where they step a soon extinguished
impression: an unpaid bill, the evidence of a missing object,
an unkept promise, the weight of a spasm in a body divided
between curiosity and constraint. He could swear his father
hadn't lived in Maceió. He'd spent a few days or weeks and
had gone, bags and all, completing new stages of a stranger's
destiny, in which irresponsibility or indifference, or an absurd hope, masked abjection.

It was from this unknown father, dogged and feckless
third-class passenger on the Lloyd or Costeira's ships, seated
always in the last cars of the Great Western trains or

squeezed into the seats of the puffing buses which made the trips between small rotting cities, that he'd inherited his vocation of writing anonymous letters. Not, evidently, because his father had written them. His nomadic life, concentrated in the attainment of small favors, dirty arrangements and illusory advantages, hadn't allowed him time to pause to observe those around him—or better, those who paraded before him, and who generally didn't keep clear or agreeable memories of his passage. But, leaving some flophouse unseen so as not to pay for the night's lodging, or unconsciously leaving the seeds of his prolongation in a prone body, he'd transmitted an invisible legacy to him. It kept him awake and vigilant on the afternoons when being part of the custom's bureaucracy allowed him long hours of reflection and leisure, or during the nights at the Old Palace, when in his solitary and rancorous consciousness there flowered the certainty that a great part of the population of Maceió was fornicating. The chief justices, the judges, the businessmen, barbers, fat proprietors of sugarcane mills and the owners of bankrupt plantations, notaries, doctors, lawyers, salesclerks, fishermen and gangsters, all were fornicating in the city that was hot despite the night and the stars, the sea and the lagoons and the wind. In this universe of nude and sweaty bodies, his father had appeared one day. He'd knocked on a door, lain in a bed, come and then left, satiated, like one who carries out a ritual or has a document stamped, relieving himself in an absence already near to death. And he'd left in the son unconsidered in that instant among instants, a heritage of wretchedness, the perpetual indecision of those who can't hear, without a shiver, a ship's whistle or the puffing of a locomotive.

He returned to the grave which was being filled. Professor Serafim Gonçalves was greeting a tiny man. Hortêncio, the businessman and numbers banker, was looking up, to better hear his lawyer's explanations. He wore a suit of linen,

whiter than the whitewash on the walls, red tie, monogrammed cambric shirt, two-toned shoes (brown and white),
and gold rimmed glasses. Professor Serafim Gonçalves ma-
neuvered his rotund belly so as to emphasize the importance
of his strategems:

"I've already appealed. It should go to the Supreme Court
this week. Let's see who'll write the opinion."

Professor Serafim Gonçalves' elucidations filled Hortêncio
with satisfaction. It was one more proof of his importance,
despite the fact that he might physically be one of the short-
est men in Alagoas, only four feet, seven inches tall. Owner
of row houses in the Harbor Warehouse neighborhood, a
plantation of coconut palms near Sweet Creek (an oil area!),
an envied businessman and numbers banker, Hortêncio lived
like a king and considered himself one of the most notable
men in the state. Busy tongues pointed him out as a chief of
the Brotherhood—and the story that he was one of the judges
of that secret and sinister tribunal, which didn't recognize
the borders between guilt and innocence, defense and re-
venge, never ceased to feed his vanity, as if it placed him on
the same august level as the magistrates. Besides, the mem-
bers of that court which decreed deaths—some in ambushes
by the roadside or in the quiet of the night, others ostenta-
tious and loud, in bars or shops or on the central streets of
the city, as if in these sacrifices there were some exemplary
intention—were, or should be, people as respectable as himself.

"And this boy's death, hey?" The question was by a fellow
with kinky hair and a sallow complexion.

"They say he had a mistress. He couldn't stand the pace."

"How many kids did he have?" The questioner made a
false grimace of compunction. On taking the streetcar, returning from the burial, he was sure to forget everything, the
words and the feigned shadow of remorse on his face. His
name was Botelho Ferro and he was a collateral descendant

of the Baron of Jaraguá. His Christian name had been lost
early in the beginning of his life. At his big hardware store
on First of March Street, he pilfered, light-fingered in the
weight and the measure. Miserly, he thought only of econo-
mizing. Since childhood he'd had only one dream—which he
didn't reveal to anyone, not even his wife—the discovery of
a buried treasure. The trials and triumphs of others were of
little concern to him. Guabiraba was close by him, conversing softly with Dr. Quintela Calvacanti, a lawyer. Dr. Men-
donça Braga, another lawyer, listened attentively. Guabiraba,
a scrounge, a ridiculous figure, intimate of the notables of
Alagoas! It was said that he had a plate always waiting in the
District Attorney's sitting room, that he could arrive at any
hour and be served. With his black and predatory eyes
shaded by thick brows, Botelho Ferro eyed Guabiraba with
rancor.

"Did you know that Dina has a new girl? She came here
yesterday from Bahia, but some say she's Pernambucan."

"No, she's from Sergipe, but she worked in Recife."

Hortêncio recalled the woman with the wine-colored bathrobe. He'd met her years before, at the beginning of his
wealth. She'd used to put a cheap smelling lotion under her
arms, and he had occupied her body like a lizard dragging
its belly across a leaf. But the two-toned shoes, shined daily
by Gonguila (the best shoeshine boy in Alagoas and star of
the carnival club The Knights of the Hills), the monogram
embroidered on his shirt by a seamstress from Pilar, the gold
rimmed glasses which had come on special order from Rio to
help him better discern his fellows, the suit of English linen
made in Recife and the ruby set off by diamonds which
adorned his left hand, were proofs of his respectability—even
more than the coconut palms advancing toward the fish traps,
the dozens of rental houses, the mansion in Farol, the bundles and boxes piled up in his warehouse, his subscription to
the Golden Book of the Knights of the Hills, the suit he'd

brought before the Federal Supreme Court or the icon which, acceding to a request by the Capitoline Monsignor, he'd presented to the church of Saint Benedict. He turned over a part of the money the numbers brought him to the authorities, perhaps it served to pay the chief justices who dispensed justice or the teachers who civilized children. The feeling of his usefulness followed him, present like the impeccable crease of his pants, and was allied with the conviction of a conspicuous cleanliness. For him, misery was dirt. His bed sheets were changed every day—a large bed of solid rosewood, legs lathe turned, considered a perfect replica of that in which Dom Pedro II had slept when he'd passed through Alagoas. And his bath was as lengthy as a bride's.

A child's cry in the distance. A bee buzzed, golden and impatient in the morning's vastness.

"Still, I got to see it. The fox was hit so many times you couldn't imagine it. It was just a mash." The speaker was a collateral relative of Góis Monteiro, a young man overly proud of his famous kin.

"And they say that Maceió is a civilized city! The foxes come out with the sun on Main Street."

He carried a pistol. But this, in truth, was part of his wardrobe, like the suspenders, the pearl tie pin and the monogrammed shirt.

"No, it wasn't on Main Street. It was on Belleview, almost on the corner by the Martyr's Palace," interrupted the reddish haired type. He was Hortêncio's bodyguard, there on duty—he hadn't known the deceased.

"So? A few meters from the Federal Interventor himself, a fox."

Botelho Ferro eyed Hortêncio with secret envy. Almost a dwarf! And yet, he'd been born lucky. It was said that he'd begun life with money from a hidden treasure, a fortune seen in a dream and dug up in an old house in Arapiraca. There were also those who attributed the origin of his capital to a stroke of luck in the numbers game due to a voodoo prayer. But Botelho Ferro agreed with those who timorously alleged that a murder lay at the roots of his life.

The lawyer felt uncomfortable once again: the gunman seemed to be observing him through half-slit eyes.

Hortêncio had already heard that morning about the fox brought down with blows in the heart of the city. Listening again, he couldn't keep other images from surfacing in his thoughts: images of men condemned by an invisible tribunal and fallen in ambush. Men who, like the fox that morning, hadn't had the slightest possibility of fleeing the sacrifice, winding up converted into bloody pulps on the paving stones or in the dust of the roads. It was as if his hand had brandished the club which had helped to bring down the fox; or the blunderbuss, the revolver, or the knife which had dropped, with frightened cries, the men marked for death and divided between innocence, suspicion, and guilt.

The men were like lost foxes ambling through the dim streets of a strange city, seeking an exit from the labyrinth of whitewash and brick. And each one of their steps brought them closer to the place where the sentence of a tribunal, unfathomable and yet sovereign and omnipresent, would be inflexibly carried out.

At the streetcar stop by the cemetery gate, the American sailor looked at the bystanders with blue eyes which seemed to shield a remote infancy. Diverting his gaze from a beggar, turned monumental by elephantiasis, Hortêncio saw the man who wrote anonymous letters. It was as if he were looking at someone condemned to death.

THE PARTY

On the night of the day that they killed the fox (or that they buried Alexandre Viana, if the reader who takes my word so prefers), there was a big party at Dina's. The versions which later spread about the city, in a circle going from the Appeals Court and the tables of the Right Place and the Colombo Bar to the hardware stores, barber shops, registry offices, and pharmacy counters, were to such a degree confused and contradictory and vulnerable that they ended up subverting the true reason for the gathering. Among those present were some of the most illustrious figures in the state, rubbing shoulders with inveterate bohemians, toothless and syphilitic, big time swindlers, prostitutes, gluttons, boozers of ability, and sailors from an American ship which had anchored in the port of Jaraguá the afternoon before. Even Guabiraba, the most renowned of freeloaders and close to the greatest notables of Alagoas, whom he invariably addressed with familiarity, was present. He brought a ravenous hunger with him, probably because he'd dreamed, during his customary nap, that the Interventor had offered a potful of crabs, seasoned with monkey-tail chile, in his honor.

According to some, the revelry was in honor of Hegecipo Caldas, who had won in the numbers lottery or was commemorating his birthday—or better, was now having it feted by his friends, since he'd spent the day of his birthday in his house on Main Street. He had been seen there wearing wooden clogs and sporting gold braided pajamas, his usual garb, worn as much for sleeping or lounging about in a rocking chair as for talking in the middle of the street, receiving friends and closing deals. For others, the straight facts were that Hegecipo Caldas had won a case before the Supreme Court (his lawyer was Professor Serafim Gonçalves) and he himself had taken the initiative of organizing the party. However, there were those who denied his presence in that festive nucleus, alleging that he hadn't even appeared at Dina's, for the simple reason that on that day he was in Coqueiro Seco or Quebrangulo with his family. Another version held that the party was spontaneous, that it didn't happen on any particular pretext, but was born from an accumulation of chance occurrences: the arrival of the American sailors (and some maintained that the boat anchored in the port was a warship in search of German submarines, while others considered it a common freighter picking up a cargo of bananas); some crab claws which had appeared at Dina's and called for the consecration of noble palates; an improvised homage to the poet Armando Wucherer who, having published his *Songs of Tedium* years before, hadn't received until then the heartfelt reverence of his friends and admirers, even though his book proved Alagoas' adherence to French symbolism. And some, tongue in cheek, let it be known that they were commemorating Guabiraba's fiftieth birthday.

The two lights of the beacon on the hill illuminated the night. Red and white. At the door of the Colombo Bar, magistrates were discussing the war and the American ship anchored in the port of Jaraguá. Ramona, one of the rare queer Alagoans, had sat down on a bench in Deodoro Square: the night promised sailors. With his mild air, Dominguinhos entered Sátiro Marques' funeral home—he wanted to know if anyone had died that evening, so he could join the wake. At the *Journal of Alagoas,* an editor armed with scissors and glue finished off the following day's edition, impiously clipping the papers from Recife, brought hours before by the Great Western train. At the *Alagoas Gazette,* old Luís Silveira, its director, was personally writing the obituary notice of the Chief of Police's mother-in-law: "Victim of a persistent illness which scoffed at all the resources of medical science, and comforted by the sacraments of the Holy Mother Church, the death yesterday at eighty-nine years of age of the revered Mrs. . . . ." In Martyrs' Square, cheap whores were hunting men, to take them to the hard planks of the Blindman's Baths. In Saint Vincent's Hospital, the old lady with swollen eyes was coming to the end of her life.

The lawyer, walking tight by the wall of the old cemetery, reached the square after waiting for an almost empty streetcar to go round the curve. From the sidewalk by the Asylum he came upon the street which, beginning at the patio by the barracks of the 20th Battalion, terminated among the beach dunes. His shoes were full of the same soft gray sand which covered the dead or was thrown by the wind into the bewildered eyes of madmen. He was not afraid in the full night. He was oppressed by the certainty that the resolution of his life—that catastrophe which would have to be the culmination of his anxious and desolate existence—would come at dawn, when the sun's rays commenced to flay the darkness. His stride was sure. His tracks dissolved in the sand in the middle of the street. He breathed the odor of the sea, heard the whispering of the coconut palms, had the momentary impression that a ship was whistling in the distance. The white and blood-red beam of the lighthouse tore the night above the roofs of the barracks and the Asylum. But these signs of voyage belonged to another universe. He was caught in the funereal sand where his shoes silently sank. He neared the house. The living room light was off: it was the agreed upon signal. Firmly, slowly, his hand pushed the unlatched door. Before closing it and feeling himself enveloped in an embrace, the lawyer again heard the arriving ship and saw the gloom of space swept by a blood-red light which could only be that of the lighthouse.

While sleep, tedium, and the desolation of the full night occupied the city, and the centipedes and bats moved freely about in the old houses, the big salon in the building where Dina's operated was all lights, music, and voices. A portrait of Getúlio Vargas, with the inscription "Only love builds for eternity," adorned the entrance hall. The sugarcane brandy they'd begun to serve was certainly the best in the world, that which assured Alagoas the privilege of eyeing with disdain the distilleries of Vitória de Santo Antão in Pernambuco or the plantations of Ceará. Flowing down the throats of those present, the "little blue" fabricated by Paulo Rolemberg on his Coruripe Plantation gave them the sensation that they'd been born in a fortunate land, deserving of universal envy.

"It's a book which should come out in the Brazilian Scenes or the Brazilian Documents collection." Professor Serafim Gonçalves was explaining his book on the Dutch colonization to the secretary of the *Journal of Alagoas*.

They had climbed the stairs leading to Dina's together. The journalist, who had offered to mention it in the Sunday edition, asked him how many pages he'd already written. He dodged. He didn't know for sure!—in his office, the notes, documents, the maps and bibliography were piling up. He added gravely: "It's work for about five hundred pages."

Guabiraba came closer to overhear the conversation.

"And Calabar, do you consider him a traitor?" The journalist licked the beer foam remaining on his lips.

"I still haven't formed my opinion in respect to that. It's
a very complicated subject, and demands a cool head. For
some, Calabar, being Brazilian—born in a colony that is—
could choose between Holland and Spain, particularly because Portugal had ceased to exist as a sovereign nation at
that time. For others, it was a betrayal, given our Iberian
origin. But I still haven't studied this matter deeply, it's very
complex, and besides, the war with Holland wasn't just economic. It was also religious, a battle between Catholicism
and Protestantism. Remember that Maurice of Nassau declared the freedom of worship, the Jews even built a big
synagogue in Recife. The Dutch didn't come here just to
look for sugar. Though I recognize the importance of the
economic factor, I disagree with Marx (you know I'm a
liberal democrat) in the all consuming predominance he
gives to it. Like Gilberto Freyre—with whom I also disagree
occasionally—I take other factors into account: racial, political, religious, sexual, even the nutritional ones."

The journalist chewed on a crab claw. Then, sucking his
teeth:

"But don't forget that the Dutch pulled a dirty trick on
Calabar, turning him over to the Portuguese, who drew-and-
quartered him. In my opinion, Calabar is a great figure, a
forerunner of our nationalism. It's not because of his being
Alagoan . . ."

Professor Serafim Gonçalves sniffled:

"It's a very delicate point in our history. And a historian,
as is my case, deals with facts and documents. Nothing of
hurried or passionate conclusions. It's because of this that
I'm taking so much time with the book."

Guabiraba was listening, snarling with impatience. Once
he'd been in Porto Calvo with some people from Rio who
took note of everything. He'd gone because one of them, a
youth a little Bahian in manner, had guaranteed him there
would be a lobster lunch. They'd seen the pillory where they

had cut up this guy Calabar, the collapsed fortifications, had heard the blue sea beating high and noisy against the afternoon. He asked for little from mankind: lunches and dinners, old clothes, small change for cigarettes and streetcar fares. Anything else would be too much.

As the journalist was rising from the table to greet Banker Hortêncio, who'd just arrived, Professor Serafim Gonçalves finished off:

"Don't forget to mention it on Sunday."

The other reassured him:

"Don't worry."

It is held to be a fact that it was during that night of revelry that the Alagoans invented whiskey with coconut milk, for the presence of the American sailors led to the joining, at certain tables, of Scotch with the famous native food and drink. No matter how, there was whiskey and coconut milk, together or separately. The best punch imaginable was served, made from the sugarcane brandy of Coruripe Plantation itself and the honey of wild bees. Many of the guests and crashers cut their drinks with pieces of cashew fruit, which was not the only snack, for on the flowered porcelain plates there reigned an abundance of crab claws, breaded or boiled and dressed with a sprig of coriander.

According to the generally accepted version, it was Professor Guedes de Miranda, director of the Law School of Alagoas and one of the greatest juridical glories of the state, who had insisted on breaded crab claws. But a few competent testimonies declared vehemently that he hadn't descended from the heights of his respectability as a man of letters to go to the party at Dina's—which was contradicted by others, also totally competent, who asserted that Professor Guedes de Miranda not only had gone to the party, in the company of his colleague Serafim Gonçalves, but that he'd proffered romantic confidences there. An anecdote of his was recalled, interrupted by the appearance of the fried mussels (or the

fried crabs, or the mussels stewed in coconut milk): "Last
month, when I was in São Paulo representing Alagoas at the
Latin American Congress of Jurists, I met a woman, with
moorish eyes and the face of a madonna, who appeared to
live on Athenian olives and old French wines." The words
were Professor Guedes de Miranda's, who'd already told the
story in a class at the university, and had repeated it in conversations with his colleagues of the Alagoan Academy of
Letters and of the Historical Institute, and even while having
lunch with the Bishop. But this anecdote, repeated and
envied, wasn't enough to document his presence at Dina's.

At the moment in which some of the dishes were making
their triumphal entry into the hall, and the steaming soup
of mussels in their shells was inebriating consciousnesses and
stomachs already captivated ·by the "little blue" from Coruripe, Armando Wucherer, the poet, was giving a dissertation
on his ethnic origins. And he guaranteed, looking about and
opening his nostrils to the aroma of the steamed prawns and
his eyes to the shrimp which seemed to swim in the coconut
milk: "The windmills of Holland turn in my blood, and
there the vineyards of the Rhine thrive."

On the other side of the table, beside Guabiraba, the
abominable Tiger Louse, notoriously connected with the
Brotherhood, was listening to him, fascinated. He was chewing, with what remained of his decayed teeth, on chunks of
sun dried meat and farofa de bolão*—the meat was sautéed
with onion and coriander and served with a farofa lovingly
fried in imported butter. Tiger Louse chewed and marveled.
From a narrow isle of discernment, he felt that these hours of
association with the important personalities of Alagoas—or
at least, with illustrious people who used ties and rings—
redeemed him from the indistinct daily routine and the

---

*A typical Brazilian dish, made from manioc flour moistened with hot
water and rapidly fried in butter.

services entrusted to his marksmanship or to his accurate and merciless hands. As there were American seamen in the city—and everyone knows that sailors, when drunk, like to fight, pull knives, break tables and chairs, and cheat the whores—his preventive and moralizing presence had been solicited. He had been received with effusion by Dina herself, who made him sit at the big table where they were celebrating Hegecipo Caldas' birthday, or the poet Armando Wucherer's winning lottery ticket.

And the best and most learned that Alagoas had to offer put away platters of mussels and fish stewed in coconut milk and fried crabs. The poet Armando Wucherer was seeking (in a language which, to Tiger Louse, was probably French, or English, or German, for the simple reason that it wasn't any language of a true Alagoan man) to instill in a seaman some idea of the richness of his state. He was explaining to him that, in truth, Alagoas floated on a subterranean lake of oil—and the day wasn't far off when, from the ships' decks, oil derricks would be seen along all the coast, mixed with the groves of coconut palms. Alagoas was a sweet land of sugar, esteemed even abroad. This was true in spite of the libels published in the Rio newspapers (they exaggerated everything, despite the Ministry of Propaganda's censorship!). They were always spreading it around that the law of the dog and the jungle reigned in Alagoas due to the frequent murders there (these had causes of a sociological nature, as Professor Serafim Gonçalves was accustomed to emphasize in court and in the classroom).

When Brazil was an empire, Alagoas already exported sugar, cotton, leather, and honey. From strange lands on the other side of the ocean came silks, calico, salted meat, wines, olive oil, medicine, cotton cloth, codfish, butter, wheat flour, ironware, and madapollam. Her brandy was impatiently sought after by the other provinces, which bought from her, besides the cotton, sugar, and leather, other local riches:

mats of rushes and reeds, great planks, beams and slabs of
wood, caroá, wool from sheep and fiber from trees, trunks to
build rafts, canoes, and yellow wax. In return, Alagoas received soap, jerky, ground coffee, metal coins, hardware, salt,
cloth, cigars, and cigarettes.

Guabiraba slowly sipped the native brandy, extolling it
with clicks of his happy, thirsty tongue. By his side, the poet
Armando Wucherer was defending his native land: a blue
and white land, and green, which a few evil or resentful
Alagoans out there were defaming. No, Alagoas wasn't a land
of murderers or short-tempered people, with revolver or
knife in the belt. And concerning the rumors that in Maceió's
jail the prisoners received more beatings than an egg-sucking
dog, they were no more than slander, spread by enemies of
the Interventor, a man of good will who was combating
communism and administrative corruption. The tobacco of
Arapiraca, for example, was superior to that of Bahia. All
this without speaking of the mussels—and he made the sailor
swallow a fried piece and drink from a deep plate the golden
broth of mussels steamed in their shells. *Good, good* . . .
approved the blond and freckled sailor, almost in a grunt.

"Only Maceió and Paris have these mussels," guaranteed
Armando Wucherer, beneath the attentive gaze of Banker
Hortêncio. He cleaned his lips with the tip of his tongue.

Thanks to Alagoas, Brazil was now a republic, like the
United States: if Marshal Deodoro da Fonseca hadn't
mounted his horse on that morning of the 15th of November in 1889, the country would still be an empire—and
perhaps he, Armando Wucherer, would be a count.

The journalist proclaimed that Alagoas had the best sugarcane brandy in the entire world. No drink on earth was
comparable to the "little blue" of Coruripe, which demanded
hors d'oeuvres of noble quality, such as crab claws or slices
of cashew fruit.

He had before him a sailor, a poor soul who had spent

weeks on a ship without seeing a woman. With his eyes alight, he confided to him (for it was a confidence, a phrase said softly and very close, in a French strewn with English and Spanish words) that Alagoas had the best whores in all Brazil. They weren't like the women from the Mangue, nor did they have the depraved habits of Recife's bitches. A little reserved, they only did it, or only liked to do it, from in front, but perhaps only in Singapore or in the South Seas did women like them exist. He pointed out a few, seen through the doorway, dancing with the sailors. Glancing about the noisy tables, Professor Serafim Gonçalves approached, holding a freshly served cup of hog plum sherbet. It could be said that the night of frolic had turned him fatter still—a grave obesity, as of magistrates or statesmen, which had girded his abdomen like a consecration or a reward.

Many of the guests had finished dinner, and there was even one who, having saved his appetite for the last courses, protested at the lack of catfish from Pilar or a good chicken in brown gravy at such a high class banquet. Some were drunk and loquacious with the drink still flowing freely, other somnolent. There were those who grabbed women to dance or simply stretched their legs with an air of animal satisfaction or of sudden indolence, and asked for a glass of wine or another cold beer, "to clean out the intestine," convinced that its passage through the bowels would be sure to contribute toward a rigorous intestinal hygiene, made necessary by the accumulation of brandies and prawns, crabs and fish, mussels and farofa de bolão.

Blinking his eyes in a gesture of impatience, Guabiraba demanded a toothpick to scrape his yellowed teeth, pitted with immense cavities. And he complained to the waiter: he'd seen *free* beer served with less foam than that!

"Great night!" the poet Armando Wucherer was commenting. In truth, to live in Alagoas was to participate in an eternal, never interrupted party. It began in the morning, on the streetcar which brought him from out by the lighthouse to the city's center. At the door of the Colombo Bar, the interminable parade: informants who saw and heard everything shook the rust from malevolent tongues; the betrayed husbands and adulteresses gave the scene a malicious tone, enlivening it even more; cold beers refreshed the throats tired from talking and commenting, speechifying and retorting. Even the beggars, ulcerated or deformed by elephantiasis, were necessary to that party which went on the entire day, against tedium and sultry weather, silence, and the fear of death. It was a party that only ended when the house lights went out and the decaying façades, still keeping some touch and semblance of lost glories, disappeared in the darkness, and the stairway steps leading to the whorehouses stopped creaking.

According to the versions which spread and changed in the following days, and the customary gossip, the party only ended at daybreak, when a group rented cars and went to take a swim in the Catolé—men and women nude, following the best Alagoan tradition, nostalgic for the earthly paradise. But according to the conversations and commentaries in the Commercial Billiards and in court, the party had come to an end right there at Dina's, almost at daybreak. Someone had suddenly shouted, while one of the Paurílio brothers was punishing the piano with a tango: "Everybody naked!" Well fed and watered men and women tore off their clothes and, in the atmosphere protected by the presence of Tiger Louse, who hadn't permitted the entrance of strangers—alleging that Dina's had been rented for the night by a select group of Alagoan society to offer homage to the officers of an American warship anchored in the port of Jaraguá—danced and shook and amused themselves until the rays of dawn lightened the sky, heralding the jovial day. The milkmen and bread deliverymen began to appear on the crooked city streets, and the streetcars, screeching on their tracks, hurried the signs of an obstinate life which would once more flourish with the sun.

In her room, the green-eyed mulatto girl loosed peals of laughter; the American sailor's caresses tickled her, and she crossed her arms over her breasts.

A graduating student suggested that, to bring the party to a close, they open some bottles of champagne. But the poet Armando Wucherer argued with the revelers, who were dazzled by his wisdom, that the occasion didn't warrant it. And, with an oratorical air, waving his arms and barely hiding a belch:

"Champagne only on a marble table, beneath a violaceous light, and next to a woman with scented underarms."

Guabiraba climbed onto a chair. He wanted to give a speech, but yielded upon being booed. Seconds later, collapsed on a sofa, he was uninhibitedly snoring away.

The salon was emptying. The cocks were announcing that day had initiated its march within the shadows. In two bouncing old jalopies, with tops down as in the Carnival processions and seeming to advance in the direction of the dawn, lighting up shacks, mudholes, yards where dogs were barking, meadows, and the crippled shrubs of the tableland, retracing the path of the fox killed the day before, a group had already arrived at the Catolé. Naked men and women splashed in the cold, enveloping, almost green water, or disappeared in the brush like pagans, laughing and squealing. And the shameless sex, transforming the men into satyrs and women into nymphs, gave Alagoas a mythological dignity in that sylvan and matinal rosy-fingered dawn.

"Beyond the Equator sin does not exist," Barlaeus had noted when writing the chronicle of the Dutch period. Then that landscape had been part of New Holland and through the rows of crooked streets and warehouses bursting with sugar passed the worst scum of the earth. Besides the Portuguese, there were Dutch, French, Scots, Englishmen, Jews,

and Germans who, sought after or hunted by the Inquisition
and other tribunals which foreshadowed the eve of the stake
or the gallows, had arrived there with their dreams and vices.
They came in search of gold and the earthly paradise, ready
to face dysentery and guerrilla warfare. The eyes of these
wayfarers recruited by the Dutch West Indies Company were
the eyes of assassins, heretics, thieves, contumacious drunkards, inveterate queers (like that Dutch captain who was
exiled to the Island of Fernando de Noronha for the crime
of sodomy and was later thrown into jail in Amsterdam),
confirmed gamblers and swindlers, sexual criminals, ruffians,
corrupt and greedy functionaries. Anything went, in that
happy land where the natives, not content with eating their
own dead, even ate Christians. On one happy occasion a
shipwreck offered them a marvelous banquet—and they devoured Bishop Dom Pedro Fernandes Sardinha, two canons
presumably fat as abbots, captains and ladies. And this prodi-
gious cannibalistic repast, in which the Indians had eaten
the West, colonizing and predatory, inhuman and ecclesiastic,
monastic and bureaucratic, erudite and militaristic, still re-
echoes today in the collective memory of the Alagoans. And
they keep in their yellow faces and in their dreams, disturbed
by the sea wind's murmur and the mosquitoes' buzzing, the
last memories of that remote past in which man, fearing from
the sky only thunderclaps and lightning bolts, was one with
nature, like the trees and animals, streams and stones. For
the human refuse fleeing the dungeon, the stake, and the
blade, America was the latrine of Europe. "Beyond the
Equator, sin does not exist," they alleged in word or in
thought; and they killed Indians and Blacks and their own
white companions. They sacked plantations, robbed warehouses and ravaged women, depositing in them, in their
burning Indian or Negro cunts, the seeds of the green or
blue eyes of those red haired and white featured Northeast-
erners of today. This permissive code had crossed the cen-

turies. And today, in Maceió's turbulent brothels, when somebody shouts "everybody naked," or wild orgies splash creek or ocean waters awakened by man's lasciviousness, a hidden tradition surfaces once again. It is a tradition of creatures faithful to the life of the flesh and the senses and suffocated by the Church and the State. And it grows and flourishes beneath the lights of those same constellations that the sage Marcgrafe used to contemplate from the observatory John Maurice of Nassau had constructed in his palace in Recife. It is as if the Alagoans momentarily remembered those remote times when everything was permitted. By the beach or in the middle of the woods, there had occurred the union between forest Indians who knew how to eat (and even ate prelates!) and the lustful Christian refugees coming from a Europe strewn with tribunals and stakes, libraries and confessionals where fat or ascetic priests also devoured the Christians, tearing forth the confessions of their abominable sins and fleshly secrets (of which the priests also dreamed). And when the Indian and the white arose satiated from the sand—and down the legs of each there ran the virginal froth of a biblical sperm—God blessed them and said: Be fruitful, and multiply, and replenish the earth, and subdue it: and have dominion over the fish of the sea, and over the fowl of the air, and over every living thing that moveth upon the earth. And God also said: Behold, I have given you every herb bearing seed, which is upon the face of all the earth, and every tree, in which is the fruit of a tree yielding seed; to you it shall be for meat. And to every beast of the earth, and to every fowl of the air, and to every thing that creepeth upon the earth, wherein there is life, I have given every green herb for meat: and it was so. And God saw everything that he had made, and, behold, it was very good.

It was still dark when Tiger Louse left the party, pretending he had to urinate. The crowing of the first roosters in the predawn light had warned him of the nearness of the hour in which his hand would once more be raised in the service of death. He'd been charged with killing the man who wrote anonymous letters. He'd already been in the Old Palace several times, walking through the dark and decaying halls stinking of piss and treading the worm-eaten stairs. Once he had even stepped in a pile of shit in the darkness. Now he would be able to find his way through that labyrinth in the blackest night. His presence at Dina's party was the anticipated answer to any suspicion. He'd do the job and be back in less than half an hour, to watch the people dancing to tangos and old Carnival songs. Upon returning, he'd be sure to hear the poet Armando Wucherer comparing the break of day to a rajah agonizing in his palace of purple and topaz.

Tiger Louse felt thirsty upon passing by the Great Western station. It was all quiet as if no train were going to leave that morning, despite the red lights in the darkness. Afterwards, he'd drink a cold beer—he said silently, like someone promising himself a reward.

The constellations had already been banished from a sky which was turning green. Clean white sheets had become dirty and wrinkled where young couples paired for the night had fornicated. Someone was dreaming that he was discovering a golden treasure hidden by the Dutch. Crabs were beginning to leave their dens. The lights of the lighthouse were extinguished: day was already showing the ships the way.

Professor Serafim Gonçalves came down the steps of Dina's shortly after Tiger Louse's departure. His fat didn't weigh on him. He felt sprightly after the sleepless night. On the sidewalk, he sniffled, then breathed deeply, and his lungs received the air of a dawn turned living and aromatic by the nearby sea. The street was deserted. The notes of the tango faded as he walked, and the party crumbled, as if it were already memory and time past. "The ship of state has already begun to sail the treacherous sea of inflation . . ." He heard the sound of steps behind him. He looked back. No one was there. A scent of unrefined sugar maintained a trace of the day's industrious movements and sounds in the desolation of the night. He raised his eyes to the sky. Not many stars. Blotches of a rusty red already opened the way for the day's clarity. When he lowered his eyes, he saw, almost in front of him, the American sailor.

As if many years before, perhaps in his infancy, he had made this date, Professor Serafim Gonçalves approached the radiant and immaculate apparition. The sailor was handsome, strong, blond. And he would leave the next day—a secret converted into distance and oblivion.

THE INTRUDER

She laughed when she made love. At first it was an almost straight, fine lipped smile, opening mutely to reveal teeth which were not as white as he would have liked. This smile expanded, and made love something happy and clear, with a trace of innocence which masked her heavy animal satisfaction. More than once, the lawyer embraced her as if to say: I don't want your love, I want only your clement and beautiful smile which, in the half shadow of the days and in the darkness of the nights, slips toward the abyss of that great joy hidden from man. When he lay upon her, holding her head with both hands and seeing her eyelids crinkle in the beginning of ecstasy, her smile would open like a radiant crease. Then he was present at that moment in which pleasure, instead of turning into a succession of cries and grunts, scooped out a little abyss of light and sweetness on the world's uncertain horizon. Articulated in a series of sounds which said nothing, if not love itself given and received—and brief and definite as a gesture, a wave held eternally in the hollow of the hand, a fragment of a falling star—the smile ceased to be merely the gift of a body inhabited by the truth of the awakened senses. Born of itself, in the two wrinkles which held it, it touched him like a beacon light or a ship's whistle—that is, as if it were something from far away, coming from oceanic and stellar distances, from the immense pure spaces situated beyond mankind's pain and sordidness. The lawyer saw himself momentarily wounded by perplexity and interrogation: why then her smile, like an unexpected synthesis of her voracious and banal body? And it was to see her smile, and to accompany the trajectory of that smile until it changed into long, sonorous joy, into the rising music of the sighs and syllables of an indecipherable language, that he began to make love with the lights on. His eyes seized upon the sudden beatitude of her face illuminated by exaltation. It was as if in the dilated wrinkles, in the quivering nose, in the agitated eyelids (and even in the streaks of penciled brows, in the narrow forehead and the tiny ears) all the emblems of life were reunited, emblems of a splendid and definitive existence which afterward was dispersed in the tiny blue veins, in the aureoles of her breasts, in the groove of her buttocks, even in the nails painted with an already cracked and fading red. As long as he was able to hear and contemplate, in the night more luminous than the very day, that laugh coming from the depths of ecstasy, he would be safe from danger and from death. Even when the laugh was transmuted into panting and silence, he felt redeemed and protected. He was a captive animal—but his cage was the eternity of a jubilation which had crossed the frontiers of sordidness and guilt, to liberate him and bring together around two tired or satisfied bodies all that was fragmented or dispersed. She would open her eyes, and in them, brown and without history, he could see only the brilliant substance of the hours, hard and unflagging as a diamond. Even in the equivocal gestures of her hands which knew how to rekindle love, searching in the ashes for the hidden fire, he encountered the mark of a purity which didn't dissolve or degenerate when her lips were sealed by a stubborn spasm. He sensed that in the world, love is a cage or an island—something which closes man in, as if he were a dangerous and condemned animal, something separate from the truth of circuses and the ocean's immensity. Love isn't life, it isn't the reality of life, reflected the lawyer, while there rested on his shoulder a head that sought to hear the beating of his heart. Love is an intruder, like a fox in the city's center or an adulterer in a conjugal bed. The world is located in a territory beyond or below love, behind walls of tedium or terror, of oblivion and indifference. It was a world of automatic gestures and identical words—while love was the mysterious language of that laugh which gave him joy and plenitude without his needing to decipher it; it was that slice of sweetness and mystery which nourished his long voyage through the shadows. The lawyer felt the arched hand searching his body for the vanished flame of desire. It was like someone kneeling before an apparently extinguished bonfire, seeking a fiery ember. Among the ashes of the world, that was love: the hidden fire of life, which only could be found by those who kneeled to discover it in the leavings of time and the refuse of empty hours. She continued searching his body for the lost spark. And he, his head resting on the high pillow, hands stretched to his knees, eyes closed like one feigning sleep, knew she had almost found what she sought. Even if it weren't the flame of love, but a coin lost among the dunes, or a needle on the spiral staircase of a lighthouse, or a perfume in the old chests containing wedding dresses and daguerrotypes, she was sure to find it—because she was search itself, in all its mute tenacity. Those who seek, find (said the lawyer to himself, wanting to stretch but not doing so, so as not to disturb with any movement the persistence of that quest), for seeking is already finding and discovery. Eyes which have dreamed the truth of life know how to make out the lost coin in the vastness of the

beach sand—and on it, seeking and finding are heads and
tails. On one side is the effigy of life, a halo, golden like a
beacon light or daybreak redeeming the night, the suffering
night degraded by man's continuous offenses. On the other
side is the image of love, two bodies conquering unfamiliar-
ity and indifference and, united within themselves, defying
horror and death. Here I am above or beyond death—said
the lawyer to himself, to his hairy nudity. Here I am fastened
to life like one who clutches a handrail so as not to fall into
the abyss of nothing. As long as this light stays lit, I shall fear
nothing: the danger is in the shadows which hide hate for
hire and the assassin's hand. Between the long and exultant
laugh and the prolonged silence, life assumes the form of
love and blazes like a sun—the brief and beautiful sun of
coins found on the beach, which the sands guard as if they
were shells or starfish. Between the gestures and words which
open the doors to the spasm and the sudden shyness of
satiated bodies, at the heart of a time as immobile as a stone,
I feel myself sheltered from death. These breasts, which hang
sweetly and weigh no more than the lightest stars, proclaim
that I'm bound to live as long as I can remain true to this
moment. I lay my head alongside this belly holding the murmur of life's entrails. Further up I hear, in the faithless heart,
the same rhythm which pulsates in the galaxies, the same
pure truth of the stars which never confide their secret to the
abyss. My mouth finally halts before your finedrawn lips.
Your teeth are not as white as I should like. You begin to
smile. Your saliva nourishes me. In your black and slippery
delta your waters moisten me. With eyes closed, I cross once
more the lie of time, descend the spiral staircases of all the
imaginary lighthouses which have illuminated my insomnia,
I pass all the great gates of dawn and, on the beach, see the
ships rocking on the sea. I advance across the dunes and
begin to dig my feet into the black and briny sand. In this
black, miasmal water end all the seas of the earth, all the

worlds beyond the world, and here all rivers end. You are like the black water of my childhood—which spoke to me of rotting shipyards and where I could still see, in the forever unfinished ships, the lacerated vertebraes of departure and voyage, while the seagulls cried as if the sun were trying to blind them. You are seminal like water and earth. You are the beginning of life, morning truth of the world begot by the night, engendered in the impassive innards of the dawn. You are beautiful like the ocean waves. My mouth travels your body like an ant. So many leagues in you, so long the path between your navel and the gloom of your pubic hairs. I spend centuries between them. Embracing your legs, I see days and nights passing, hear the cocks crowing, ships whining like dogs. Wagon wheels flay the secrecy of the sultry heat that makes the afternoon horizon waver. I kiss your breasts, at once bridal and maternal. Redeemed by the nuptial beauty of your body, purified by your complete and pure forms, I'm blinded by tears. My weeping swells the rivers and the seas, flays the mist, hides the dirty sidewalks of harbor warehouses, fades the semaphore flags, scars the mountains. Only now am I aware that men cry for joy. Only now have I learned that joy is the great river where mankind swims like fish. It was your apparently fumbling hands which showed me the way of the water. Your voice thickened by love rouses me from my millennial dream. Awakened, I begin in you my slow and painstaking ant's day. Your industrious tongue touches me like the highest wave in the height of the whitecapped sea. Hoarse words come from your throat when, sucked up by the resplendent day, you see the sheets become sand and dunes, and a gelatinous sea full of algae pours from your womb. The evening becomes a viscous night. And again day. And once more night. And is again beyond day and night, where time is only a wrinkled sheet on an unmade bed, and life's rhythm is regulated by two panting breaths. I whirl about you as if you were a planet.

You receive the light of my wise and irrational love. You are wet by the sweat of my agony. The shadow of my uncertainty encompasses you. I descend once more to your hidden wealth, there where you are gift and secret, hunger and clamor. Immersed in this dark matrix, I see your body dance like a ship on the turgid waves. I leave the hieroglyphs of my passion inscribed on your back. I kiss your feet, so they will remember me when I am dust and ruins and epitaph. I suck your breasts, twin fountains of infinite life. My fingers close your lids, so that you see nothing and are only remembrance and plenitude between battlements. I regret in silence that your hair isn't fine and long and luminous as a comet's tail. And again I feel you growing within me, a long and generous plant, a landscape full of hours and places. Your laugh rises in the air like banners, ignites the evening lights, deposits in me the emblems of the eternity which will still be mine when, riddled by gunshots, I fall dead on the paving stones . . .

THE WINDOW

A window opened in Saint Vincent's Hospital, and the nun who suffered from insomnia felt the gentle night wind on her face—a face without age, uncreased by wrinkles. The breeze coming from the sea refreshed her.

Once again she was at *her* window, erect and immobile. She didn't need to stoop to see the night's desolation. And as the light was off in the room, she wouldn't be seen from outside. She was a shadow among shadows in the predawn silence—a silence of wind and water, in the city risen from tidal pools and full of water names: Mill Race, Harbor Warehouse, Land's End, Lake Orchard, Watering Spot, The Well, Sweet Creek, Rock Spring, Bend in the River.

As every night, she'd gotten up after a few hours of brief and compact sleep which, having dispersed, seemed always to have exhausted all her reserves of indolence and fatigue. She'd put on her habit and begun her peregrination through the deserted and badly illuminated halls until establishing herself at the window. It was as if a frontier existed between her awakened consciousness and the night. Already feeling in her body the strength for her daily work, she contemplated the night's end as if the dream were in the things. Or as if the things themselves were dreams: the hospital sidewalk, the empty square, the humpbacked houses, the front of the jail where pale creatures rotted while staring at the bars, the sentries who observed the succession of days and nights from the barracks, the two pictures (a Sacred Heart and a portrait of Getúlio Vargas) decorating the room.

Although she came every night to that window, like someone seeking a refuge, or only mechanically obeying a habit—or wanting to sniff, with nostrils accustomed to the smell of disinfectant, the sea wind which crossed the city, heading toward lagoons and mountain grottos—she couldn't accept the fact that it was another night in time being vanquished in desolation and shadow. To her, it was the same morning unfolding before her eyes, an untouchable and irreplaceable substance, even when some unexpected figure, such as a drunk or a sleepless dog, crossed the empty square. The silence of the spent night didn't signify time's flow, the stars' march across God's sky. Time had stopped, the hours were not advancing, the snakes slept in their nests, groves of coconut trees stretched unmoving by the dunes, the fish slept in the sea and the wasps in their homes. In the interminable night of those who suffer from insomnia, time is not a step or a wave, a fragment thrown into the glacial torrent cutting its way between constellations, but rather the unblinking eye of a screech owl crouched on a cornice, ironically looking out upon the immutable darkness of an upside down eternity. When day came, that morning would deflate like a balloon, to be filled again in the moment when she, no longer tired enough to sleep, would get up once more in the darkness, feet seeking her old sandals.

The day before, she'd gone to the mortuary, on the excuse that she was looking for a nurse, but in truth wanting to see the face of the man who had committed suicide. It was a sharp face, like a fox's. It had become swollen and yellowish

like the hide of an egg-eating snake, and death had conferred
a certain irrationality upon it, causing the sister to think
about the fox clubbed to death that very morning in the
city center. It had been the nurse who had told her the story,
the same one she had pretended to be looking for in the
mortuary, and who was her customary informant. From him
she'd learned that the suicide, a married man, had had a
mistress—but on seeing his face, she observed in it no sign
of worldly possessions. Like all the dead, he was only poverty
and privation, snatched forever from what had been love
and ecstasy, folly or perplexity. She'd learned that suicides
didn't go to heaven, that their souls were cast into the depths
of hell. But she'd also learned that, thanks to divine mercy,
there was room for salvation even in the most infinitesimal
particle of time. Was Alexandre Viana condemned to a fiery
hell (and why not one of ice and cold?) or could he be found,
at that moment, in the great waiting room which was purgatory, abiding until the end of time, when the gates of paradise would be opened unto him? Death was ambiguous. From
his swollen face there came no enlightenment or sign of
journey whatsoever. Grasping her rosary, she again thought
about that frigid region which consumed souls for all eternity. Hell was a white and motionless desert she had once
seen at a movie in Penedo. No wolf wandered that wilder-
ness, now flat as a table covered by the whitest cloth, now
sinuous and undulating but stripped of any vibration in its
slow and untouchable curves. Hell was a luminous emptiness, an immaculate and boundless glacier, dug and extended beneath a sky also white and starless, in a time made
from the vacuum of nights and abolished days. It was also
silence—not the silence of the frozen or rotting dead, of
souls forever buried in oblivion, but the silence of things
themselves reduced to their essence of stone hidden in the
heart of ice, of forms fading on an insubstantial horizon,
long space concealed from itself, and where there would

never echo the prolonged howl of a starving or solitary wolf, or the panting of a terrified man. She started, as if she felt the cold accumulated on that movie screen coming across the years like a great unburdened wind. That sometimes dubious vision of an inferno illuminated by its whiteness fixed itself in the core of her insomnia as if trying to rescue her from loneliness. But God didn't know hell, even though He'd created it. Hell was undulating nothingness, petrified silence, absolute cold.

The sister thought of Alexandre Viana as if he had been a fox which had been pursued by invisible hunters in the distant early morning and finally sacrificed. So, in truth, were all creatures: harassed by a great hunter who cut them down so they could enter the true garden of life. In her morning routine through the wards, she was accustomed to meeting the humbled beasts. That woman with black spots all over her body and the prostitute who exhibited her wine-colored bathrobe as if she were wearing liturgical vestments were already marked for death, like Alexandre Viana at the moment he'd taken a mistress, the fox when seen by the guard at the police post, or the teamster who had gone for a swim in the sea and drowned.

She shivered, as if the sea wind had chilled her. Every being in the world walked toward his death. She was also an animal promised to the absolute cold. But her own death didn't weigh upon her. She kept it within her—something like the rosary beads her fingers explored almost mechanically every day or the scapular hanging from her neck. It meant the end of her insomnia. A patient and docile animal, silent and reflective, she would sleep eternally in God's warm lap, free of all the questions she didn't dare ask the chaplain or the mother superior. Falling upon her, death would be as sweet and merciful as the rain.

Her attention was concentrated on the deaths of others, in that hospital where many entered already bearing on their

faces the mark of their imminent end. As a child, she'd
avoided killing ants; she'd walked with caution, eyeing the
ground. Once she'd cried at seeing a dead bird. Taken as a
boarder to study at the convent school, she'd become accustomed to silence and solitude. At that time she was still a
child, she didn't know or couldn't choose—but only accept
the path which others, thinking to know her better, had
pointed out, as if she were a little ant of God. She had become a nun. She'd begun to wear a wedding ring on the left
hand, like a married woman. She was the bride of Christ.
As a novice, she'd presumed that her future existence would
be spent in a church school among girls learning to em-
broider and playing ring around the rosy, supervising flower
arrangements in the illuminated chapel. Thus, she'd live as
a spectator, far from the world's misery and abjection, removed from humiliation and pain, praying for the salvation
of millions of unknown creatures. But soon those faceless
sinners to whom she dedicated her prayers had been replaced.

And there before her was Alexandre Viana's yellowish
face, thin as a fox's snout. God hadn't wanted her to remain
at the side of life, in the convent which at dusk was the
swallow's refuge. At Saint Vincent's Hospital she partici-
pated almost silently—so sparing was she with words and
gestures—in the world's misery and corruption. She cared
for women whose innards were slowly decaying, for men
with dropsy, children with hookworm and old rheumatics
who breathed like ancient and damaged bellows. At certain
moments, she was assaulted by the thought that the world
was vile and ugly, that perhaps she was dealing with only a
rough sketch by God, a mere divine smudge. However, she
banished the confused and audacious idea and, squeezing
the rosary beads with her fingers, accepted once again that
everything, from a constellation to a venereal disease had
meaning. Life had meaning, as absurd or sinuous as it might

appear. The practice of charity had meaning. Her insomnia had meaning, guiding her in the night's passing to an island of silence where, awakened and refreshed from her daily toil, she could unravel her thoughts as if she were a rosary. Even her doubts and questions had to mean something.

She was at the window one morning when a group of winos and bohemians coming from a binge or fish banquet passed nearby. Her ears filled with the lovely tune which seemed to rise, elegant and with dew moistened words, to the skies where the constellations were disappearing:

> The everlasting is a mysterious bloom,
> it smells sweet, yet has no perfume.
> I sent a bouquet to my one and only,
> but it was made from painted daisies
> and shone like Venus in the morning sky.
> Good-bye girl, child of the morning dew . . .

Those nightbirds, with their singing, were beyond disease and death, insomnia and paralyzed time. But what did she know about happenings beyond the hospital walls or the world's fine phrases? Her life had been love and acceptance from the beginning. She pitied even the ants her feet inadvertently crushed. Never had her adolescent eyes come to rest on a young man. Her first and only love had been invisible and yet present in everything. He had become the meaning of her life, had warmed her frail cold body, had imposed difficult and servile tasks upon her. Once, she'd had to remove the bedpan used by the prostitute with the wine-colored bathrobe, who had a diseased uterus. But in this and other moments of her life as a hospital nurse she was never attacked by the idea that she was building up merit for divine reward. Surrounded by beings violated by disease and clinging to the certainty of life even when the last agony hung clearly about them, she accepted the evidence that the hospital was death's waiting room. The human refuse lying

beneath the grimy sheets of the ward beds were comparable
to the migrants piled up by floods and droughts in the patios
and on the platforms of railway stations. They were leaving,
not knowing to where nor on whose order. Little people,
unimportant people, nobodies, they ambled about like sleep-
walkers or Wandering Jews. Night and day were all they
had of their own. Who would they meet at the end of the
line? A hacienda foreman? God? The nun shivered, remembering suddenly the other worlds which excluded the images
of pain and wandering. Beyond the wall of the jail and the
barracks sidewalk, the hunchbacked houses and the night's
darkness, there lay the world of those who didn't seek or
await anyone or anything, and there also stretched the world
of those who waited for the appearance of the fox in the
early dawn light in order to club it to death. Then this fox
changed into a man, assumed the form of Alexandre Viana's
cadaver in the mortuary, and the nun experienced a certain
disorientation upon feeling in her very depths where the
answers to her insomniac questions slumbered, the existence
of a link between the death of a fox and the sacrifice of a
man, by suicide or by assassination.

When she'd entered the convent, coming from a tiny two-
roomed house in the middle of a rice field (she had shared
a bed with an older sister), she had been most impressed by
the size of the classrooms and hallways. The old building,
with its several floors and flights of stairs and high severe
furniture had the majestic air of a palace. During her first
days as a boarder, she had gotten lost several times in the
empty rooms and corridors. It was as if she were in a labyrinth. Yes, the world was a labyrinth. Leaning out one of the
high windows, she had sought to orient herself: below, there
was an enclosed garden, with a tiled fountain in the center.
Red and white dahlias curved under the weight of their own
beauty. A blooming poinsettia stained the space between
two pilasters with crimson. Birds sang and flew: coderos,

tanagers, hummingbirds, xexéus, thrushes, all the birds of her childhood. Tumblebugs droned. Lost in the labyrinth, she had looked down on God's garden, full of roses and azaleas. What steps must her feet go up or down to reach it? Which stairway led to that fountain of pure water, to the golden marigolds which, shining in the morning sun, refused to remember death, to the lilies that proclaimed the eternal glory of God?

Now she was at the other window which, over the years of insomnia, had finally become *her* window, since that of the convent had been only the site of a provisional peep. She was thinking about creatures lost in the labyrinth of life, like the drowned teamster, Alexandre Viana, the woman with black spots, the prostitute with the wine-colored bathrobe, and so many others. Do those who are lost reach the window from where God's garden can be seen? Where, in the gloom of the halls and corridors of whatever old palace debased by bats and centipedes, is the stairway to salvation? And why were some saved and redeemed, and others cast into the damnation of a hell of ice and fire, denial and cruelty? She was a poor hospital nun, ignorant and spent by insomnia, and she couldn't or didn't know how to respond to such questions. She clung to her rosary so as not to be bruised by questions beyond her capacity to understand, to understand a world where she doled out her life, carrying out the most burdensome tasks and seeking to bring to faith and hope those who already flaunted the emblem of death.

Sister. . . . She was sister to the suicide, to the leper, to the woman with the wine-colored bathrobe, to the guards who had brought down the fox, to the afflicted piled up in train stations. This fraternity tied her to evil, to terror and death. It made her an accomplice to everything. The hand raised to brandish the club which had destroyed the fox was also hers. She had pulled the trigger of Alexandre Viana's revolver. No, she wasn't removed from the world, her nun's

habit didn't separate her from things and beings. She was a
link in the immense chain, a bead of the world's rosary. God
hadn't called her to retire from life, but to contain it in her
trembling heart like an open wound. She was certain there
was a passage between the window (any window, even that
from which she observed the final purity of the night) and
the garden at the end of the labyrinth.

That predawn frozen in time, which was neither today nor
yesterday and appeared more a mimicry of eternity, was sure
to open with the break of day to the sun which warms men
and small birds and shines on the trails of ants. But perhaps
the world was only God's dream. It hadn't even been created
yet, it existed simply as a divine plan or intention. The fox,
the guards who brandished clubs, Alexandre Viana's swollen
face, the splotches on the neck of the woman with leprosy,
the diseases of the woman in the wine-colored bathrobe—all
this was a dream. Her own insomnia was part of God's
dream.

After lingering over this thought, the nun put it out of
her mind. No, God had already created the world, dividing
light from shadow, separating the waters and the earth, plac-
ing luminaries in the firmament of heaven to show the ages,
days, and years, making man in his own likeness and image,
male and female. God didn't dream. God was reality. God
was eternal insomnia: from His window He contemplated
all his creations, the fox and the guard armed with a club,
the suicide and the leper, the centipede and the fish lodged
in the drowned teamster's stomach, the dahlias heavy with
so much beauty and the swallows nesting under the eaves
of the convent at nightfall.

It was a terrible God who had created, at the same time,
sleep and insomnia, the ship and the tempest, the hunter
and the hunted, drought and cloudburst, the fox and the
guard who had crushed the beautiful savage snout with a
club, the snout of an animal lost in the labyrinth of the city,

like an innocent far from paradise. And she, a poor nun, bowed before God's inscrutable designs and accepted, in the silence of her insomnia, the eternal mystery of the world.

In the daybreak silence, the cock crowed. It was a cock of golden plumage, resplendent, and his ruby red comb rivalled the flaming glory of dawn. Magnificent, exultant, he sang jubilantly in the splendor of the awakening day, rousing those who slept and dreamed, proclaiming the glory of God while his spurs raked the whole earth.

An enormously fat man passed by on the sidewalk, accompanied by a blond sailor.

Minutes later, new steps resounded on the hospital sidewalk. It was the lawyer who had spent the night with a married woman whose husband had traveled to Bahia. In the deserted square, he was chewing over the phrasing of the caveats he would present to the Appeals Court. A word shimmered in his head. He'd decided to refer to the tribunal as venerable. The word was of Latin origin, it couldn't fail to be appreciated by the judges. Tribunal! It also came from Latin, as he'd been taught in Recife by his professor of Roman Law. The lawyer remembered the almost completely sleepless night, the profusion of gestures and caresses beneath the light of the lamp. He liked to make love with the lights on, especially when the woman in question was married— it was as if the evidence of guilt and betrayal, or the shadow of danger, nourished his pleasure. For an instant, the white sheet covering them had seemed cold and funereal as a shroud. Satiated, shyness had hushed them. The fear of what they had done in the endless sleepless night had left scars of reserve and silence in both. They had turned out the light. Turned to the wall, she hunched up a body which fatigue had emptied of offerings, and sought shelter in him for her back that had again become pure and intact after being violated by ecstasy. He'd bent his legs to accommodate her in a semblance of protection—and there was something demented in the blowing of the wind along the beach, agitating the foliage of the coconut palms, and in the tumult of the black rats in the ceiling. The whistle of a steamship coming into port at that moment, cutting the gloom, interrupted her half sleep. Imprisoned in his eternal present, he had felt her quiver in his arms like a big invisible bird. Now, having reached the New Street Sidewalk, and recalling that house where he spent his nights but always left before the dawn, he wondered: Am I a scoundrel, or isn't it important? Could it be that all men are like me, and that the purest and most self-righteous of them are no more than perverse creatures hiding unconfessable guilt? Near the Alagoan Lyceum, the roosters' crowing calmed him. It was a promise that the world would become luminous like the room where he'd spent the night in the delirious vigil of his guilty love. With the coming of the sun, his punishment (a conspiracy of night and shadow) would be postponed.

The nun closed the window.

THE NIGHT AND THE SHIPS

He'd gone to bed earlier than usual on the night of the fox's death. After dinner he'd begun to feel a certain indisposition—perhaps the fact that he hadn't visited his mother's grave was troubling him. A few steps would have been enough to carry out the little ritual. From the window of his room, he watched the blackness which coincided with the dark sea and the lights of the anchored ships (one of them was an American warship, and blond, beer drinking sailors, dressed in white, had spread throughout the downtown bars and the fleshpots of Hay Street and Jaraguá). He sought to banish the unsettling thought from his mind, though he was devoid of remorse or simple regret. Even if he were to go to the cemetery again, as had happened before, his wandering steps would never bring him near his mother's grave.

Day was already beginning to break when the Old Palace's stairway groaned. Cautious steps were approaching his dreams, and on the frontier between waking and sleeping, the conjectures flowed.

Perhaps it was his father who, finally surrendering to the

necessity of a place to die, had renounced the short trips and
shady deals, the fallacy of profits in small transactions and
confidence games aggrandized by his imagination. Maybe he
was there on the other side of the door, at the end of a
lengthy path on which false or precarious information or
suppositions had sidetracked him more than once, ready to
confess his error—and perhaps his villainy—to his unknown
son, already a man like himself, full of resentment and
rancor.

Like dogs that have a presentiment of the supreme instant
of agony, and have before their eyes all the fantastic lights
of a life lived close to the ground, there was his father, presumably resolved to occupy the place in his son's heart until
now free and inaccessible. The short trips had worn him out.
He was tired of the long waits on docks, on station benches
where the destitute and defeated farm families waited for
imaginary trains to carry them south, tired of sitting in
government office waiting rooms where they didn't pay the
least attention to him, and the dim and fraudulent hours
passed as if time walked backwards like a crab. His sole
possessions were his old shoes that slapped when he walked,
a shabby blue serge suit (to tell the truth, he had stolen it
from a roommate in Sergipe), and some reluctantly given
letters of recommendation. These had yellowed, unused, in
his pockets, either because he couldn't locate the addresses
or because they didn't exist, had been replaced by other
bureaucrats, or had refused to see him. This was all he carried, like a crystallization of his hopes and waiting. He'd
finally learned that everything was passage. The roads and
dialogues had vanished among eroded geographies, rotting
gangplanks, and curious or enigmatic beings. There he was, on
the other side of the door, with his hangdog look. He had
searched for months or perhaps years for that drop of sperm
squeezed from a body already affected by several simul-
taneous diseases (a back pain, a steady dripping which

stained his grimy shorts, a cough that kept him from sleeping
and disturbed the other flophouse lodgers) and transformed
into the man who was his heir. As if he had anything to
bequeath other than his shoddy air, the clothes pilfered from
a craps player in Aracaju, the letters of introduction crumbling in his pockets, and a train ticket obtained in a police
station and never used. It was his father. And his promise
of intimacy already germinated an unavoidable question—
he would want to know where his mother was buried, for in
the search for the lost son he'd learned both that she had
died and that the boy had been interned in an orphanage
and had later studied accounting.

The vehemence of the blows on the door carried something imperative which didn't lend itself to the image or
version of a father seeking a son. He admitted that there was
a certain inexplicable purport of judgment in the visit. No,
it wasn't his father. His father had disappeared forever, between the mythic and the anecdotal, most likely he'd come to
an end in a flophouse or a charity hospital in Rio or São
Paulo. Perhaps he had only known how to proceed in small
towns, where the people, even unknown or hostile, or fearful
of his sometimes viscous contact, assured him the maneuver-
ing room suitable to his insignificant ambitions. The me-
tropolis had swallowed him up forever, without it ever having crossed his mind, muddied by fatigue and bitterness, that
once in Maceió he'd engendered, as if he were some negli-
gent god, a creature in his own likeness and image.

Without his having risen from the bed to turn on the
light, a milky clarity was invading the room. The door burst
open. They seized him, and soon he was descending the steps
of the Old Palace's creaking stairway.

The night had dispersed, dissolving the ships and revealing the rain blackened roofs. Outdoors, a whitewash bril-
liancy was shimmering away. All the passersby wore white
suits, of a whiteness similar to that of the American sailors'

uniforms—though, in the doorway of a lottery shop belong-
ing to Banker Hortêncio, where they also booked the numbers game, an old man dressed in blue serge stood immobile.
The doors of the hardware stores and haberdasheries were
already open. Guabiraba's too short pants were white. Street
urchins and vendors of jawbreakers and pieces of peeled
sugarcane contemplated a movie poster. Gonguila and the
other shoeshine boys were bent over white shoes—Banker
Hortêncio's two-toned shoes were the only exception. Standing by his side, Professor Serafim Gonçalves waited, pretending not to see a beggar in white rags stretching a hand toward him.

Neither of the men who flanked him (and both wore dark
glasses, more to hide their faces than to protect them from
the dazzling sun) had uttered a word. But he knew where
he was being taken. What most surprised him was that, in
all his life, from the moment when the sounds from his
mother's room had awakened him until now—with all the
stages at the orphanage, in the accounting course, at the
warehouse counter taking care of freight or shipments, or
in his room, writing anonymous letters—it had never crossed
his mind that the moment of this visit was coming nearer.
His name figured in a black book like those in the archives.
They couldn't fail to come looking for him. He wouldn't
be forgotten. Sooner or later his name would make itself
clear and legible among scrawls and rubber stamps, inkstains
and erasures born from bribes and secret arrangements.

Now he was crossing the threshold of the sooty-fronted
building which had appeared once in one of his dreams—
a half musical, half lugubrious dream, in which he went to
the beach with some other orphanage boys, and there found
a tiny white and rose-colored shell in the sand. It grew un-
controllably in his hands and later everyone entered a cage
whose key was lost. The waiting room was full of expectant
creatures. Some had the timorous gaze of those who fear

something like an affront or violence. Others could barely keep themselves afoot, or sagged worn-out on the benches, blinking in their struggle to keep awake. They were poor people tired from waiting, used to grievances and supplications—like his father in the police stations where they gave free train tickets to the afflicted, or in the government office waiting rooms where it was possible to obtain, at the cost of a lot of insistence, a letter of recommendation which soon yellowed in one's pockets. But he didn't stop to look at these people, anxious or persecuted or perhaps already condemned. All that registered on his retinas was a chance image, in which faces and clothes piled up in a half-gloom, for he passed through several doors and thinly partitioned rooms and was taken to a place probably located in the rear of the building. A few bars reminded him of circus cages seen in his childhood (or in a childhod dream, when he was in the orphanage). In one of those real or imaginary cages an old and stinking lion, annoyed by flies, cast baleful eyes upon the visitors, even if they were orphan children. It was a fastidious look of disgust, as if there were something repellent in the human species which made it hate a world long since become nebulous with lethargy and vomit.

He was left in a large room illuminated by a dim bulb in a green lampshade. On the wall, a portrait of Getúlio Vargas. At first he thought the room was empty. But, like someone rising from beneath a table, probably after picking up a fallen requisition, a shape gained form and consistency in the apparently empty chair, became present in the sweat running down its neck, the cardiac victim's respiration, in the pen scratching at a piece of paper.

"Your name?"

He was nobody, he had no name. Or he'd lost it on one of the orphanage excursions, or on the way to the cemetery when he'd gone to Alexandre Viana's burial. Or he'd forgotten it. He could allege that his letters had neither signa-

ture nor return address: they were anonymous. Yes, he was
a man without a name, a residue of life like the thousands
or millions of creatures who occupied the small or large
cities, filling the streetcars, the buses, trucks, trains, and
ships, or asking for something difficult or impossible to be
obtained, a train ticket or a letter of recommendation, internment in an orphanage or a hospital, or a discharge.

"My name is nobody." He could have said that, if at that
instant it had occurred to him that his lack or absence or
non-right to a name would fit in a phrase which abolished
any human profile. But how to say it? The lampshade covering the bulb was no longer green. It had turned red, intriguing him, shocking him, since the world's changes didn't
correspond to magic or miracles. With what voice to say his
non-name? He knew that, if he opened his mouth, nothing
would be articulated. And thus, as he had no name, he had
no voice, neither letter nor signal to turn him present or
acceptable to the world order. In truth, his lips had been
sealed for millennia. In a rockbound dawn, when the whim
of the gods had already determined his anonymity, his silence hung in the stalactite grottos, a wedding of animal and
vegetable materials, like a crystallized drop or a bat.

He said nothing. At the bottom of a consciousness still
constrained by the interrupted sleep, he knew that, whatever
his answers were, they wouldn't merit belief, wouldn't
reecho in his interrogator's mind; they would slip away like
a coin which, bouncing from stone to stone, ends up finding
the gutter. He was in the kingdom of questions and not of
answers. Even if he had a name, it wouldn't be accepted, but
rather refused as a falsehood or an alibi, or accepted condi-
tionally, in a succession of half-doubts, until the investigations and inquiries confirmed them. He was in the kingdom
of questions which already rose up with the answers tied or
glued to the question marks.

He saw himself alone, abandoned. He found himself again

among questions without answers. Someone had hung up
the cord of the bulb, which now glowed from on high, hiding his interrogator's face. Now, the lampshade was yellow,
the same color as the bulb, but this transformation no longer
perturbed him. He'd become habituated to the metamor-
phoses—and these, changed into routine, might even pass un-
noticed.

"Why didn't you visit your mother's grave?"

Despite no word having left his mouth, the phlegmatic
scribe was writing his answer, in a calligraphical operation
requiring hours, or perhaps even days, for while he was
scratching the paper with his pen, the cathedral bells rang
several times, even a dirge for the deceased, the cemetery
gate grated open, ships whistled in the distance, goatsuckers
flew low, and the chamber where he found himself—and
which now expanded, now contracted, in accordance with
bureaucratic convenience—alternately knew light and darkness.

"And the bed of the Emperor, Dom Pedro II?"

The clerk scratched at the paper.

"Let all who see this know that, in the year 1859, the province of Alagoas was visited by His Majesty Dom Pedro II
and the Most Serene Dona Teresa Cristina. First, the Emperor stopped in the city of Penedo, from there going on to
visit the Paulo Afonso Falls. Afterwards, he took ship for
Bahia, in order to meet the Empress. And exactly on the
last day of that Year of Our Lord, the Emperor and his most
esteemed consort landed in Maceió. After disembarking,
they went to Our Lady of Joy where they attended a most
solemn *Te Deum* in thanksgiving for the safe voyage they
had made. The All Mighty having been thanked, Dom
Pedro II and Dona Teresa Cristina headed to the imperial
residence (which time, the Republic, bats and centipedes
would someday turn into the decaying Old Palace). An *ad
hoc* commission, named by Dr. Manoel Pinto de Souza

Dantas, provincial president, had decorated the palace so that the visitors would feel as if in the royal residence at São Cristóvão. The bed destined for the imperial couple was vast, solemn, and nuptial. In prime wood, beautifully worked by experienced craftsmen, and in the softness of its duck down mattress, it reconciled the greatness of an Empire which extended like a continent from the Amazon to the River Plate with the secrets of conjugal intimacy. During the eleven days spent in the province, the Emperor visited the old city of Alagoas, the towns of Santa Luzia do Norte, Pilar (already famous for its excellent catfish), Porto de Pedras, and Porto Calvo, a textile mill which bore witness to the region's vertiginous economic development, and the former military colony of Leopoldina. A grand ball, which remained forever incrusted in our forefathers' memories, like a jewel, was given for the imperial couple. Gentlemen, with dazzling suits and uniforms, and ladies, gay and enchanting in their dresses of silk and satin, filled the stately hall of the provincial Legislative Assembly on the eve of the Emperor's departure. His Majesty didn't hide his enthusiasm for Alagoas' progress nor for the beauties of its formerly cannibalistic countryside, and he was even thinking of composing a sonnet about Maceió's beaches or the palm encircled lagoons. Their Majesties so liked the ball and the noble reception, and the sincerity and worth of the people—and the dainties and cakes and native sweets which held their own even when served with the renowned wines of Portugal and France—that upon returning to the imperial capital, Dom Pedro II rewarded several Alagoan gentlemen. The owner of the building which had been transformed into the imperial residence received, in exchange for the magnificent lodgings, the title of Baron of Jaraguá, while, of his three cronies, one was named commander of the Order of Christ and the other two attained the status of officers of the Imperial Order of the Rose. Those responsible for the success of the ball—they had waltzed until dawn, and a diplomat of the imperial entourage had compared Maceió with Versailles!—were also singled out by the monarch's generosity. The two Barons, of Atalaia and of Jequiá, were raised to baron with grandeur. The Appellate Judge, the Supreme Commander, and the Port Captain (a retired navy commander) became commanders of the Imperial Order of the Rose, while the Inspector of the General Treasury and the Public Health Inspector were named officers of the same order. On the Municipal Judge of Maceió and the Juvenile Court Judge, His Majesty conferred the insignia and garb of the Imperial Order of the Rose. The Inspector of Public Instruction and a gentleman named Raposo were awarded the insignia and garb of the Order of Christ. After Their Majesties' departure, the Baron of Jaraguá locked up the quarters where the royal couple had stayed. Everyone knows that Dom Pedro II was no saint and that, where conjugal fidelity was concerned, he followed in his father's footsteps. Besides, at the time of his felicitous voyage to the province of Alagoas, it was reckoned to be about sixteen years since he'd contracted marriage to the Most Serene Teresa Cristina. However, he was then about thirty-four years of age, in full enjoyment of his masculine vitality (and moreover had ingested, during those happy days, some victuals of incontestable aphrodisiacal qualities, such as mollusks, crabs, and shrimp). The hypothesis was not to be scorned, therefore, that during his visit to Maceió and sleeping in such a nuptial bed, he might have carried out his most sacred marital duties—so neglected or poorly fulfilled in the imperial capital! Thus, there was no shortage of motives for putting that bed of solid rosewood—lovingly worked by cabinet makers who, under the knowing guidance of the Baron of Jaraguá, had sought to imitate or recreate the style of Dom João IV—out of the reach of unsuitable or indecorous curiosities or phrases with double meanings, together with the bureau, the wardrobe, and the mirror, which were also true works of art and the quintessence of Alagoan rococo. Time passed; and the years were hidden, faded, in the transcripts of archived certificates, in the epitaphs on cemetery tombstones, in the dog Latin of the sacristies."

In the dark night, goatsuckers continued frightening skittish horses on the roads travelled by drunkards and muledrivers.

And the tides rose and receded.

Sooty spider webs blackened walls.

Cattle hawks soared in the dry air.

The crack of a .44 caliber faded into silence. At nightfall, a man fell dead. And the fences marched across the land, marking new boundaries.

As the days rolled by, clothes moths and termites proliferated in the chests and wardrobes smelling of lavender and ancient portraits and gnawed the brides' nightgowns.

New signs and insignias were covered with rust.

And the wind blew.

And it rained.

And the cloud bursts inundated the valleys, leveling houses and fields.

And in the end man's hopes became deception and disappointment, shadow and time past.

A rifle shot reechoed at dawn. The blood of a fox stained the floor of the universe.

Saints appeared in the hinterland, promising land for everyone. But the land had owners. There were those who brought suit, and the crosses by the roadsides, marking the locations of ambushes, substituted for the geodetic survey markers.

In the imaginary night which, in the movie theaters, merged with the real night, the Alagoans saw the films of Charlie Chaplin, Griffith's *The Broken Blossom,* Lubitsch's

Madame du Barry, Cecil B. de Mille's *The Ten Commandments* and *The King of Kings,* Stroheim's *The Merry Widow,* and King Vidor's *Hallelujah;* and assassins' eyes flooded with tears before the invented poignancy.

The ships whistled in the night sustained by the constellations. And the souls of the English seamen dead of yellow fever sought their lost flag in the wind's path.

The sauba ants rested sweetly on slimy islands.

And the ancient breech and muzzle loading pistols were replaced by modern automatic ones.

The first Fords advanced, dancing disjointedly down dusty streets which were old horse paths widened by progress, crushing chickens with their high and slender tires, frightening pigs and dogs.

One day an Airpost plane crossed the sky of Alagoas in the conquest of the South Atlantic—and at night its lights were vagrant sonorous stars among sedentary constellations.

Then the Graf Zeppelin appeared among the clouds, and the Alagoans, armed or pacific, sensed that life was the flowing of a perennial river and that the world's changes were accumulating in the years torn from the calendar.

The sea planes began to land on Mundaú Lagoon, flying over tidal pools and rotting ships.

Again the moon swelled the dark sea, and life's routine continued engendering, among gestures and words of oblique or illusory meaning, mold and despair, tedium and death.

An artisan, time was weaving its own labyrinthic lacework.

The films of Tom Mix and Buck Jones arrived.

Suddenly, the sweet November rains, watering cashew trees, fell on roofs and yards, frightening vultures and washing the damaged locomotives in the Great Western yard.

The number of automobiles wheezing to a stop at the Texaco stations increased.

In the Church of the Rosary, the apple-cheeked angels

heard neither the sins of men streaming forth in the confessionals nor the squeaking of bats hanging from the vaulted ceiling.

At twilight, the whores, smelling of jasmine, leaned from the windows of the houses on Sin Street.

There was wind, moon, and sun; and rains to water the mango trees; and cries and words of love; and on days of rain and vengeance blood ran in the streets, staining the paving stones and men's hands. Piano movers made musical the streets marked by death. They were English pianos, Broadwood or Studard. They came in the stinking ships which also brought codfish from Newfoundland, woolen fashions, vaseline, and chinaware. And the young ladies played the *Tales from the Vienna Woods*.

Marijuana plants blossomed inebriatingly in fenced off lots.

Treacherous memories forged life's designs.

Men to kill and men to die followed one another.

On certain afternoons, people climbed stairways to hear, at jury trials, the prosecutor and the defense attorney's harangues—and, on the prisoners' bench, the murderer had the sensation of finding himself in a theater, as if the metaphors, robes, and moist sputterings had raised his personal case to a noble and polemic level, higher than his sordid and mechanical existence.

White light. Eclipse. Red light. The beacon illuminated the blind and migratory night. Its incandescent lights swept the ocean, tinged the sky and the crests of waves, reached the ships, but didn't manage to pass through the closed and bolted windows hiding spiders and centipedes, bats and dreams and the secrets of men held to their beds like owls stuck on cornices and changed into walls of stone.

Blue and red, the semaphore flags raised there on the hilltop, by the lighthouse keeper's house, announced the ships as, in the old days, muzzle loading cannon had proclaimed, in the dazzling air lacerated by the seagulls' flights, the steamers' arrival. These steamers, emissaries of the universe, had brought silks and perfumes from Europe, the Empire's new laws, and news of the war with Paraguay.

While the truncated conical tower of the lighthouse guarded, in its manioc whiteness, the door to the ocean sea washed by palpitating waves, Maceió slept its coal black sleep: a sleep above or below, this or that side of the innumerable sounds and the wind's murmur, the damaged shipyards and the abundant rivers, the flour mills and fish traps, the St. Elmo's fire resting like giant fluttering butterflies on ships' masts and dung-colored roofs, the crowing of roosters surprised by the disgusted dawn and the black islets in the lagoon.

On a Good Friday, an Alagoan atheist, to win a bet made at a tripe stew banquet and meant to prove the nonexistence of God, put a lit cigarette between the fingers of the image of Our Dead Lord on display in the cathedral. He was left bent and twisted that very night due to an apoplectic stroke, and he saw in his punishment the evidence that God existed and that Jesus Christ had been crucified to save all mankind. When he passed in the processions, wearing a surplice black as his sins, already pardoned for all the endless ages, he symbolized divine mercy even more than the saints in their biers. In Maceió, only God forgives.

But before the cars and the gallons of Gargoyle gasoline, before Lillian Gish moving, languorous and angelical, on the Capitolio's screen and the clatter of balls and cues in the Commercial Billiards, it was ordained that an Alagoan of the purest stock, the celebrated Marshal Deodoro da Fonseca, God rest his soul, would raise his sword against the Emperor and topple the Empire. Perhaps this caused Dom Pedro II, in the embittered sonnet-writing old age of an exiled king, to revise his opinion as to the nobility of the Alagoan man. Another Alagoan, the proud and courageous Marshal Flori-

ano Peixoto (a fervent patriot, he was ready one day to wel-
come the English with gunshot), succeeded Deodoro da Fonseca, certainly causing the latter to reexamine his opinion of
his fellow Alagoans.

Since this dawn of the Republic, which still today fills
Alagoan schoolchildren with pride, not to mention the first-
class wastrels and deadbeats who spend the afternoons in the
brothels, drinking beer and exchanging amenities, no Alagoan has managed to reach the presidency of the Republic.
However, one of its most illustrious sons, General Pedro
Aurélio de Góis Monteiro (who helped bring down the Old
Republic and will surely help, at the opportune moment, to
destroy the New State, of which he was one of the able
architects) has all the extraordinary qualities of statesman-
ship necessary to govern this great country.

In the whirlpool of time, the palace where the imperial
couple had slept lost its splendor and, termite by termite
and bat by bat, was reduced to an enormous ruin, with
rooms full of leaks and musty obscurities where marijuana
smokers took refuge. The doors had warped; the scum of
the city climbed the crumbling steps of its creaking staircases, despite the presence of some agencies and radio repair
shops here and there, and a few rooms occupied by students
and clerks.

The bed where the royal couple had slept (and made
love?) disappeared. The descendants of the Baron of Jaraguá,
or his mere distant collateral relatives, had in truth become
a rabble. The men were tied to humble employments at
windows or counters or giving injections from door to door.
The women lived taking in sewing, working as midwives,
or as confectioners skilled in cracknels, cornbread, sweetmeats, and jellyrolls. Some people thought they had sold the
bed for a song to an antique or junk dealer from Recife. He,
according to the story, had made a killing reselling it,
months later, to a papal count in São Paulo, in a deal in-

cluding pieces of a set of tableware from the Dutch West Indies Company, a carbine, and a chamber pot. For others, the bed had perished in a fire, after passing some years in an alcove of the Martyr's Palace. It had been requisitioned by the government after the proclamation of the Republic, perhaps in the same week when, in a steamer paradoxically called the *Alagoas*, the banished Emperor navigated off the Alagoan coast, on his way to the fair lands of France.

As truth and falsehood are, after all, flour from the same sack, and life is intrigue or confusion, there were those who had seen the bed in the most diverse places: in a whorehouse, in a hovel, in the Imperial Museum in Petrópolis, at an auction in Rio. Some guaranteed that the bed, with the passage of time, had ended up in Banker Hortêncio's manor house, where he slept in it. Complete blind foolishness: that was a replica which Hortêncio had had made based on information supplied by the President of the Alagoas Historical Institute, particularly in reference to the handturned legs. The real bed had disappeared.

"And Dom Pedro's bed?"

When he, after finishing the accounting course, had arranged that job in Jaraguá (he'd learned all the secrets of the import-export business) and had gone to live in the Old Palace, he hadn't seen any bed at all. He'd rented an empty room and had furnished it with a cheap bed purchased on the installment plan, a wardrobe, a table and a chair. To ask him the whereabouts of Dom Pedro's bed was the same as asking him where his father was. He'd never seen them, had heard neither of one nor the other.

"Where's your father?

How to explain that he'd never known him? As a child, he had been pointed out as the son of a loose woman. Or the son of a whore, to be exact. His father had been only an instant between soiled sheets. A wanderer, he'd vanished beyond the night and the ships, beyond alleys and hillsides;

he'd crossed islands inhabited by clayeaters and fields culti-
vated by eaters of ants; he'd disappeared behind cashew trees
and marijuana farms, behind dunes and waves, briny warehouses overflown by hoarse seagulls and the grottoes of crabs.
He was a creature without a name, an outsider accustomed
to fleeing flophouses on the sly and begging free tickets for
his journeys by train and ship to some Godforsaken where-
ever, always out of sight and hearing. Certainly he also, one
day at dawn, had been torn from his guilty sleep and taken
to a room where they had grilled him with unanswerable
questions and offended him.

"Do you recognize this handwriting?"

How to recognize it, if it wasn't really his handwriting,
but a disguise, an almost always clumsy reproduction of
newsprint which protected his anonymity. It was as if, during Carnival, he'd used a mask. Now he was alone, in a
cubical as narrow and stuffy as a urinal. He was dizzied by
the stench of rotting fish. The sea had gone rotten. A sink
dripped. Or was it the flushing of a damaged toilet. Or the
wheezing of a ship gathering forces in the roaring of the
waves. Or a Great Western locomotive, blowing with thirst
in the switching yard.

The night was giving birth to words. Or was it the howl
of a fox, free and beautiful and secure against death?

"Talk."

Sink ship toilet fox. The words swelled, had a hide which
wrinkled.

"Asshole."

The sink the slut. The night gave birth to seagulls. The
words stank of low tide, disappeared in the darkness like
islands drunk by the lake of the night.

"Talk, you son of a bitch."

On the black and triumphant waters of the sea which was
drinking the constellations, the ships advanced heavily, as if

they only carried death. Birds screeched—or they were the cries of men, in cells which had abolished the clear daylight hours.

"Talk, you lousy cur."

He pissed. And the black piss flowed across the cell, crossed the hall, reached the walls of the Martyr's Palace, extended, clamorous and interminable, to the ocean.

Suddenly, the roar of motorcycles starting up filled the silence. He sensed that now he would be able to speak. He murmured a few words: *Maceió, cemetery, noble fellow citizen, customs, my father, virtuous consort.* Each one of the words was clear, unmistakable, a sonority in which there entered a thing or a landscape. The rumble of the motorcycles was steadily increasing. *Your reverence? Your excellency? Bishop?* Even if he screamed until hoarse, no one would hear him. Walls rose up to isolate him from the world. Then he slept, his lids now heavy, now light and sensitive to the scraping of a table in the hot night or to the cries tearing the silence.

He dreamed: the orphanage children blamed him for having lost the key to the cage. Again he awakened, with his eyes burning, and a sharp pain in his stomach. He didn't remember having eaten. Perhaps he was hungry. Then he remembered that, moments before (or days before), in the cubicle illuminated by a dim bulb (or a bright bulb), he'd complained of hunger.

"Talk, shithead."

He dreamed again: he was walking on the beach, by the waters. All the ships were painted white. The sea itself was white. He doubled over with the pain which clawed at his entrails—a pain he didn't deserve, great as his sins might be. The blood ran from his open mouth which could no longer scream, and from his quivering nostrils. The thick liquid joined the fine water of his tears. Without words, he thought:

My God. But it was less an appeal or request for help than a startled interjection. There was no God where he was—it was the stinking cage of humanity.

He slept. He dreamed he was awake. He heard his mother's cautious steps nearing his bed, sensed again in his nostrils that scent at once loved and detested, stiffened when a slightly tremulous hand pulled at the cretonne sheet. But this time his mother hadn't brought a night light. The light illuminating the room came from the anchored ships. Later, his father fled wearing seven league boots, vanished in the dark of the night.

Once more he dreamed he was sleeping. He dreamed he was awake. Dreamed that he slept. He awakened. He heard the flowing of a river without water and the ships advancing against the gloom, defying the shadow. In one of those ships plowing the coagulated sea, Guabiraba was leaving. Pursued by creditors, he was fleeing Maceió. Despite the distance and the dark night, he was able to see him, immobile on the deck, blinking. Dressed entirely in white, he would wander the face of the earth, lose himself among the crossroads of the world.

"If you want to eat, you've got to tell us your name, prick."

They'd explained to him (but who were they?) that the names of the recipients had to appear, compulsorily, in the food requisitions. Rigorous control mechanisms were put into action, so that the victuals were not misappropriated by venal or corrupt functionaries. The papers, registered, passed through several sections, receiving opinions and stamps, giving rise to inspections and investigations. Besides, no cash outlay could exceed the funds available. In many cases the process took weeks, years, perhaps centuries to be expedited. The higher authorities fought against the administration's archaic structure, tried to simplify it and speed it up, but the clerks never stopped scratching with their pens at papers which wind and dust were turning yellow.

Nameless, he'd returned to the cubicle—he had neither voice nor identity to order lunch, or dinner, or the coffee he liked to drink with lots of sugar and white bread.

He heard the whistling of ships which would never again return, lost among the white glaciers of hell.

He heard the motorcycle engines. He tried to lie down, but there was no bed—and if there were, the space, equal to that of a latrine, wouldn't hold it. He sat on the cement floor, hugging his legs, which had gone numb. The stomach pains increased. It was no longer hunger he felt; it was something similar, but distinct—as where he found himself was similar to a latrine, despite not having a toilet. His eyelids weighed heavily. When he closed his eyes, and sleep began to absorb him into nothingness, the clarity of millions of suns set in lampshades of mutable colors forced him to keep awake, beneath a ceiling of firmament lacerated by lightning and thunder. Sleep was an evasion, an escape like that of his father when leaving a flophouse without paying the bill. It was necessary that he keep awake; awake and nameless, awake and hungry, awake and powerless to answer the questions dripping like water from the broken sink. His hands were heavy, as if, cupped together, they held a pink and white conch shell that he'd found on the beach as an orphanage child.

His eyes stopped seeing, clouded by a darkness riddled by lightning bolts. He fell, while the pain churning his stomach descended to his groin. The cement floor was cold, like the wind or death. His lids weighed more and more—a weight of tears or blood clinging to the lashes. He felt himself held by strong and invisible hands which were trying to raise him up, but his knees wouldn't obey, they doubled with each attempt. A humming filled his ears. In his dizzy lightheadedness, cries mixed with the snarling of motorcycles. The pain rose to his lungs and his blocked nostrils dilated in search of air. Something swelled up within him, like a balloon. He vomited the hot thick liquid which had filled his mouth. He tried to speak. The words wouldn't leave his heavy tongue. He sucked in his belly, once more in pain, held his stomach with both hands. My God. He was beyond hope and pity, where loneliness came to an end. In that black cold territory his mouth moved uselessly: his grunts could never capture the shattered words. His right hand swelled. In a light made of shadows, his fright increased. With that now paralyzed hand he'd crossed the silence and the loneliness. He'd written letters. *My distinguished fellow citizen is being betrayed by his wife. A friend.* And lying in bed, eyes closed, mind seeking to recapture the image of a dark-skinned, green-eyed girl, he'd used to empty himself in vertigo and ecstasy, thanks to that hand which had learned how to open for him, in the darkness, the path of love. A stench of shit came to his now cleared nostrils—a cage smell, of a stinking lion chasing away flies, a brief exhalation of a filthy snout. With his hard, bloodshot eyes, he tried to make out the forms which were approaching him, perhaps to put him on his feet or to sit him up, or to stretch him out on the cement floor, as he no longer could keep track of his position, which varied from moment to moment in the vertiginous darkness. The wind entered by the cracks in the windows, threw open crumbling doors. Or it wasn't the wind, but rather the intermittent howling of caged animals promising vengeance, even from the other side of death and nothingness. An itching swarm of ants climbed up his numb and swollen legs. The wind. The ants. The sound of water falling in the basin. The ants changed into newsprint, formed words multiplied into phrases. *To His Excellency, President Getúlio Vargas, Catete Palace. Abusing your Excellency's trust, the Federal Interventor of the State of*

Alagoas . . . The pain coming from his groin obliged him to squat down. The words had dissolved, had become tiny black ants on the cement floor.

He shivered from the cold, enclosed by the white night which was freezing him. His teeth chattered. His legs had gone dead, it was as if they'd been amputated. A rusty drool ran from his mouth. Later, a suffocating heat enveloped him.

During an interval between the clarity and the darkness, he felt himself upside down. Perhaps it was hunger, or something that, beyond hunger, flayed his entrails. He was suspended from the ceiling like a light. Rust covered bars expanded in the shadows, and bats sucking up gelatinous time hung from worm-eaten ceilings like damaged lamps. There were centipedes under all the beds. Maceió was one big cemetery. The world turned. The world was a top spinning on the sidewalk. Perhaps it was thirst. He heard waves. And ships. He walked a shell strewn beach. He was soothed by the modulation of the abyssal sea. A hand, anonymous like his own, was writing in charcoal on a wall, *Down with the New State.*

Suddenly, the clamor of the motorcycles diminished to become the rattling sound of a key in a lock, or of a door being forced open.

He'd inexplicably returned to his room in the Old Palace without it having been necessary to cross the street, full of sun though it was night, or climb all those stairs. Was somebody pounding on the door? Was it his father? Or an American sailor? In the darkness, he surrendered himself to the fact that, on the other side of the door, there was somebody determined to enter his room. Fear took hold of him. He didn't want to scream or demand explanations of the mysterious visitor. He only wanted the noise at the door to belong to the already inaudible and untouchable substance of his dissipated nightmare. Covered with sweat, he hunched up in bed. His legs were trembling. He wanted to urinate. *Eminent fellow citizen . . . Alexandre Viana didn't commit suicide. He was assassinated by the Brotherhood. The police know but don't . . .*

Then the door opened.

He closed his eyes—even if he'd wanted to scream, the words wouldn't have left his mouth. For an infinitesimal second, while he listened to the breathing that filled the room, he ceased to be human. His insensate love of life transformed him into an animal, perhaps into a fox. An animal, innocent and in danger, he was becoming visible in the dawning day. It was the day of the hunter that was emerging from the shadows. Between the panic and the pain flaring in his guts which caused him to empty himself and spun him upside down once more, between the frozen light and the mist, the silence and the death rattle, he was vertiginously leaving himself behind, and the cauterizing pain itself was becoming distant, taking him with it or leaving him behind, abandoned in the absolute darkness.